She shook ... **a crazy wor** ... **a loud whisper.**

"No. What I think is that I want to make love to you. And I think you want to make love to me. And if we make love, I think we both know that it's not going to be a casual encounter that either of us is just going to forget about. So we need to regroup. That's what I think."

His comment struck a nerve, and she nodded. "I should probably warn you that I've never done well with relationships," Catherine said.

Noah smiled. "Well, there's a first time for everything."

She smiled back. "I really had a great time tonight."

"So did I." He moved to her side and grabbed her hand, entwining their fingers tightly together.

"Walk me to the door," he said as he turned in the direction of the exit.

When they reached the entranceway, Noah turned. His gaze danced over her face before he leaned forward and pressed a kiss to her cheek, his lips lingering. His touch ignited a raging flame deep within her.

He pressed his hand to her cheek, his fingers trailing the line of her profile. She leaned into his palm, closing her eyes as she relished the intensity of his touch. And then he kissed her.

Dear Reader,

How exciting is this? More Stallions! Finding that new branch to the Stallion family tree came with some challenges, but I have so much love for this family that it was well worth the effort. And, of course, there could be no Stallion story without that foundation of family, friends and faith.

Much like his Dallas cousins, Noah Stallion is the consummate big brother. He's loving, protective and generous. He's also a stern, no-nonsense taskmaster and he'll melt your heart. He's partnered with the indomitable Catherine Moore, a woman who knows what she wants and who won't let anything keep her from achieving her goals. Together, they are fire and fire, so prepare for some serious heat!

Stallion Magic embraces some of my favorite things and places, so I hope you'll enjoy the journey.

I cannot say thank you enough for your support. I am humbled by all the love you keep showing me, my characters and our stories.

Until the next time, please take care and may God's blessings be with you always.

With much love,

Deborah Fletcher Mello

deborahmello.blogspot.com

Stallion MAGIC

DEBORAH FLETCHER MELLO

(H) **HARLEQUIN**® KIMANI™ ROMANCE

To Big Daddy
For keeping me on track.
I love you!

Recycling programs
for this product may
not exist in your area.

ISBN-13: 978-0-373-86406-5

Stallion Magic

HARLEQUIN®
www.Harlequin.com

Printed in U.S.A.

Deborah Fletcher Mello has been writing since forever and can't imagine herself doing anything else. Her first romance novel, *Take Me to Heart*, earned her a 2004 Romance Slam Jam Emma Award nomination for Best New Author, and in 2009, she won an RT Reviewers' Choice Award for her ninth novel, *Tame a Wild Stallion*. She continues to create unique story lines and memorable characters with each new book. Born and raised in Connecticut, Deborah now considers home to be wherever the moment moves her.

Books by Deborah Fletcher Mello

Harlequin Kimani Romance

In the Light of Love
Always Means Forever
To Love a Stallion
Tame a Wild Stallion
Lost in a Stallion's Arms
Promises to a Stallion
Seduced by a Stallion
Forever a Stallion
Passionate Premiere
Truly Yours
Hearts Afire
Twelve Days of Pleasure
My Stallion Heart
Stallion Magic

Visit the Author Profile page at Harlequin.com for more titles.

THE STALLION FAMILY TREE

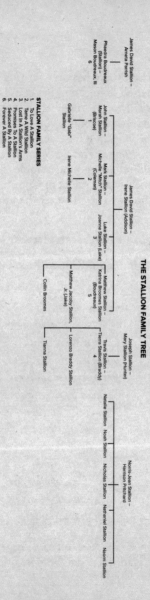

James David Stallion – Arneta Parrish

James David Stallion – Irene Stallion (Addison)

Joseph Stallion – Mary Stallion (Hunter)

Phaedra Boudreaux (Stallion) – Mason Boudreaux, III
6

John Stallion – Marah Stallion (Briscoe)
1
Gabrielle "Gabi" Stallion

Mark Stallion – Michelle "Mitch" Stallion (Coleman)
2
Irene Michelle Stallion

Luke Stallion – Joanne Stallion (Luke)
3

Matthew Broomes Stallion – Katrina Broomes Stallion (Boudreaux)
5
Matthew Jacoby Stallion, Jr. (Jake)
Collin Broomes

Travis Stallion (Brady)
4
Lorenzo Brady Stallion
Tianna Stallion

Norris-Jean Stallion – Harrison Pritchard

Natalie Stallion   Noah Stallion   Nicholas Stallion   Nathaniel Stallion   Naomi Stallion

STALLION FAMILY SERIES

1. To Love A Stallion
2. Tame A Wild Stallion
3. Lost In A Stallion's Arms
4. Promises To A Stallion
5. Seduced By A Stallion
6. Forever A Stallion

Chapter 1

Noah Stallion adjusted his necktie, taking one last glance at his reflection in the mirror that decorated the men's restroom. The expensive designer suit he wore fit him well and as he stared at his reflection he couldn't help but think that despite his initial reservations his investment in the silk garment had been well worth the money.

He took a deep breath. This would be his third interview with the company who'd actually sought him out. He'd been surprised when the head of their Human Resources department had first called to inquire about his availability. She'd been fully aware of his credentials even though she'd never laid eyes on his résumé.

Since he had not been in the market for a new

job he hadn't thought twice about hanging up on the
woman. But she'd persisted, calling back to convince
him to at least meet with their management team to
discuss the opportunity. After some serious consideration he'd acquiesced but not before his two sisters had pointed out that blessings didn't just drop
in your lap without a good reason. That first meeting had led to this one, an interview with the company's chief operating officer, and Noah still wasn't
sure if he was even all that interested in the position.

As he exited the men's room and moved back
to the front foyer toward the reception desk he just
missed colliding with an attractive woman, whose
own attention was focused on her iPad. His reflexes
were sharp as he grabbed her by the shoulders, pre-
venting what could have been a painful accident. As
he steadied himself, and her, she apologized at the
same time as he did.

"Oh, excuse me!"

"I'm so sorry!"

Noah smiled brightly. The beautiful woman met the
look he was giving her with one of her own. Her brown
eyes were wide and darted back and forth across his
face as she stared. Her own face was flushed, color
warming her dimpled cheeks.

"Are you okay?" he questioned, concern tinting
his tone.

Her voice was rich, the alto timbre ringing warmly
between them. "I'm fine. I should have been paying
attention to where I was going. Thank you for catching me," she said.

Noah nodded. "I'm glad I could keep both of us from falling," he said, his smile widening as he held the intense gaze she was giving him.

She smiled back before breaking eye contact. "You have a good day," she said as she eased past him and moved down the hallway.

For a brief moment Noah forgot where he was and why he was there, wanting to continue to stare after her. The woman was stunning. As she sauntered down the hall he couldn't help but admire the side to side strut of her full hips. The red pantsuit she wore flattered her voluptuous figure. Catching himself, he took a deep breath then quickly turned around, almost missing the look the woman tossed him over her shoulder.

Noah moved to the reception desk. A young girl with deep blue eyes and a porcelain-white complexion greeted him by name. She then gestured for him to take a seat on a blue-and-gray-striped upholstered sofa. He took a step, then hesitated, turning back around.

"Do you know who that woman was in the red suit? She headed in that direction." He pointed behind him.

The girl shook her head. "I'm sorry, Mr. Stallion. I didn't see anyone, so I'm not sure who you mean."

"Oh, well," Noah said with a slight shrug of his shoulders. He moved to take a seat. As he settled himself comfortably, he took a deep breath, holding it for a brief moment before blowing it past his full lips. Minutes passed as he waited, watching people come and go. A mountain of memories were suddenly spinning through his head, intruding on his thoughts about his interview.

A lot had happened in the past year since his mother's passing. Norris Jean Stallion had died in her sleep, quietly slipping away on her own terms. Much like she'd lived her life, there'd been little fanfare, her children not even knowing she'd been ill. With Norris Jean's death, her youngest child, his sister Natalie, had found her way home for the first time in twelve years, reestablishing contact with her family. And then there'd been the discovery that they had cousins they'd never known about, a branch of Stallions on a family tree thought to have only been a mere limb. Family support suddenly extended beyond their Utah ties and the abundance of it had been phenomenal. Since then he'd married off his sister Natalie and imagined Naomi wouldn't be too far behind. Now he was being offered an amazing opportunity and a beautiful woman had just crossed his path. Noah couldn't help but smile, thinking just how good his life was.

Noah extended his hand in greeting. "Frederick Ross, it's good to see you again," he said, a look of surprise washing over his expression.

Frederick Ross smiled broadly. "Noah Stallion. It's been a while. We've come a long way since our days at Bountiful High School."

Both men paused in a quick moment of reflection as Frederick gestured for Noah to take a seat. The former high school athletes were meeting in the boardroom of Fly High Dot Com, a multi-million-dollar aircraft leasing company. The high-end decor was a mix of polished woods and expensive leathers. Framed photographs of the company's fleet of expensive planes decorated the walls.

Noah slowly eyed the images one by one. He echoed the sentiment. "I don't think either of us ever imagined going from that muddy football field at Bountiful to the likes of this."

Frederick nodded. "I know I didn't but I'm glad we're here. So, what do you know about our company?"

"I know that Fly High has a worldwide fleet of over one thousand private jets. By far the largest of any other company. You've proven yourself to be an industry leader in safety and security. You employ a team of some seven thousand employees. You're currently the number two private leasing company worldwide and well on your way to taking the top spot because of your exceptional customer service and your fly share programs.

"Forbes named Fly High one of the top ten fastest growing companies and its owner the most elusive self-made millionaire next to that guy with the biotech firm in Georgia. In fact, the press has deemed Cat Moore the hardest interview to nab in history. So what's he like to work for?"

A wry smile crossed Frederick's face. The chief operating officer tilted his head as he met Noah's questioning stare. "Not at all what you expect. And I'm impressed that you did your homework," he said.

Noah nodded. He leaned forward in his seat. "I always come prepared and I know you've established an imposing security team. So I'm not sure how I can improve upon that."

"I need someone with your skillset to manage that team as well as help us expand as the company continues to grow. Your résumé is impressive. You have a stellar military background and your tenure with the Salt Lake City police department shows that you are more than capable of taking the lead. All you have to do is say yes and the job is yours."

The man continued to extol Noah's virtues and the benefits of working for a private firm as opposed to his current government job. Then he made note of the starting salary and Noah's eyes widened.

"We have some negotiating room if you demand more," Frederick said. "Management is looking to take the company public so we can negotiate stock options and a host of other benefits, including a company car and free air travel. You'll be based here but we'll require some of your time in our New York and Atlanta offices, so you'll have to travel. I really believe you would be a great asset to our organization or I wouldn't have recommended you."

Noah's eyebrows lifted slightly. "You recommended me? I'm surprised."

"Don't be. I actually ran into one of your brothers and he told me what you did. After a little research I knew you'd be the perfect fit."

"I'll need some time to think about it," Noah said, his mind beginning to race.

Frederick nodded. "You'll receive a formal offer from us in the next forty-eight hours. Then I can give you another seven days to mull it over. But after that I'll need an answer."

"I appreciate that," Noah responded.

"So, are you going to the class reunion?" Frederick questioned, changing the subject. He leaned back in his leather executive's chair, folding his hands together in his lap.

Noah shrugged, his full lips pulling into a warm smile. "I've been thinking about it. It'll be good to see everybody again."

"I was thinking the same thing although I'm not sure that I'll be in town that weekend. But if I can work it into my schedule, I think I might stop by. It'll be good to pound fists with the guys again."

For a few brief moments the two men walked memory lane, recalling their days together on the football and track teams. Both were laughing heartily when Noah glanced down to his wristwatch.

"I hate to do this but I need to get back to the station. It was good to see you, Frederick. I appreciate you offering me this opportunity," Noah said again. "I'll be in touch."

Both men came to their feet and shook hands. "I really hope you'll come on board," Frederick reiterated. "I promise that working here will be quite the experience."

"You'll hear from me soon," Noah promised.

Walking to the elevator, the old acquaintances were still knee deep in conversation when the door opened on the conveyor. Noah stopped short when he caught sight of the beautiful woman from earlier. Once again she was lost in the digital screen of her electronic device.

Catherine Moore stepped out of the elevator. She came to an abrupt stop as the two men moved in front of her. She took a quick glance one way and then the other before settling her eyes on Noah Stallion's face. A bright smile widened across her own.

"Why do you look familiar?" she questioned, eyeing Noah curiously.

"We did just run into each other. Literally," he said, amusement crossing over his expression.

She shook her head, tossing Frederick a brief look. "No, we've met before. I'm sure of it."

Frederick laughed. "Noah Stallion, allow me to introduce you to Cat Moore, CEO and owner of Fly High Dot Com. Catherine Moore, this is Noah Stallion. You probably remember him from Bountiful High School. We all graduated together."

Noah's eyes widened, surprise registering on his face. "Catherine Moore? Head cheerleader, Catherine Moore?"

"Now that was a long time ago!" Catherine laughed. She repeated his name once and then a second time, hesitating briefly as she tried to put more familiarity to the face. She finally nodded. "Noah Stallion. Our senior year you played football for the Bountiful Braves, second string quarterback, right? Everyone used to wonder how you made the team."

"I was quick and fast on my feet, that's how I made the team," Noah said as he shook his head.

Catherine nodded, the memories coming back to her. "Actually, you were really good. People wondered why you didn't play before senior year. So, why didn't you play before then?" she asked.

He smiled. "Family obligations."

She nodded, studying the look that glistened in his dark eyes. "You were kind of nerdy with glasses back then. And really thin!"

Noah laughed. "I was not *that* thin."

Her eyes skated the length of his body, and she thought that he'd definitely filled out quite nicely. She bit down against her bottom lip, her eyes glistening as she lifted her gaze back to his. "Didn't we have a class together?" she asked.

"We actually had two classes together. Biology and Spanish. You sat two rows behind me in Miss Garcia's Spanish class."

Catherine's smile widened. "Miss Garcia! I did not like that woman!" she exclaimed.

Noah chuckled with understanding. "I don't think many of us did. But that was a long time ago."

Catherine extended her hand to shake his. His grip was strong, his palm and fingers warm and soft. His touch was electric, sending a shiver of heat down her spine. She took a deep breath before speaking again.

"Well, it was nice to see you again, Noah Stallion."

"The pleasure was all mine, Catherine," he answered, his smile warm and endearing.

Frederick patted him on the back. "We'll talk soon, Noah," he said.

Catherine and Frederick both stood watching as the elevator doors closed on Noah's exit. She then turned her gaze toward Frederick. "Catching up with your old pals now?"

"Something like that. He was interviewing for the security position."

She nodded, finding that tidbit of information interesting.

"Are you going to the high school reunion? Noah was just saying that he might go and I was thinking about it."

Catherine shrugged her narrow shoulders. "I really hadn't thought about it. Too much on my mind with the IPO process. Speaking of, how are we doing with all the reports the underwriters need?"

"Still on schedule."

She nodded, then without another word, headed in the opposite direction.

Behind the closed doors of her office, Catherine moved to the window, hoping for one last glimpse of Noah Stallion as he maneuvered through the parking lot to his car. She caught sight of him just as he reached his vehicle. She stood staring as he removed his suit jacket and laid it on his backseat.

Gone were the wire-framed glasses, and there was nothing nerdy, thin or awkward about the man. The former high school jock had blossomed nicely, she thought, her gaze following as he slid into the driver's seat and started the engine. Seconds later he pulled into traffic and disappeared from sight.

Catherine moved to the bookcase behind her desk, searching the tomes that lined the shelves. Her friends had sent her a package recently, trying to entice her to attend their high school reunion. When she finally found what she was looking for, a copy of their high school yearbook, she pulled it into her hands and placed it on top of the desk. She flipped through the pages quickly until she found Noah's yearbook picture. There had been no change to his smile and the shimmer in his dark eyes, both just as they'd been when he'd been a teen. Catherine felt herself grinning foolishly as she flipped from one photo to another: Noah and the football team, Noah running track, Noah on stage in a theater production, Noah's senior portrait.

She reached for her cell phone, hitting the speed dial for her best friend Camille Trent. "Hey, do you remember Noah Stallion?" she asked immediately when the line was answered.

Camille laughed. "Yeah, he's a police detective now. One of his brothers plays professional football and the other is a doctor. And he has two sisters. Why?"

"I was just asking."

"You don't call me in the middle of the afternoon to just ask a question like that for no good reason. Something must've made you inquire. Spill it!"

"Apparently he's interviewing for a job here in the Utah office."

"I haven't seen him since his mother's funeral."

"You went to his mother's funeral?"

"My mother and his mother went to the same church. I took mama to the funeral."

There was a pregnant pause as Catherine fell into her own thoughts, staring back out the window. "I think I might go to the class reunion after all," she finally noted.

Camille laughed again, the hearty snicker ringing loudly through the receiver. "You liked what you saw, didn't you?"

Catherine laughed with her. "He's all right."

"Girl, you know that man is *foine*! So are his brothers."

"You ever date any of them?"

"No, I never dated Noah."

"I said any of them..."

"You meant Noah."

"Goodbye, Camille!"

"Are you flying back to New York or will you be in town for a while longer?"

"I'm boarding a plane in thirty minutes. I've got tickets to the theater tomorrow, so I'm headed home."

"You have a dozen homes. It's hard to keep up!"

Catherine smiled. "I've got to go."

"You do that," Camille said, still giggling. "And you might want to call Crystal. I think she might have gone out with him," she said as she disconnected the line.

As the call went dead, Catherine shook her head. Friends since the crib, she, Camille and Crystal had cheered together in high school. They'd been joined at the hip and had been dubbed the Three Cs by their classmates. Catherine thought of Camille and Crystal as the sisters she'd never had and trusted them both with everything. There'd been a code of conduct they'd established early in their history, rules they lived by. No dating men the others had dated being one of them.

With a deep breath, she pushed the speed dial for Crystal Baxter, the other leg in their trio. As the device rang in Catherine's ear she wished a silent prayer that she, too, had never dated the likes of Noah Stallion.

Chapter 2

The day had been a long one, and when Noah pulled up to his Arlington Drive home, he wasn't expecting to see his brother's Jaguar sitting in front of his garage door. Inside the house, the television was blaring Monday-night football on his big-screen television. Voices echoed from the kitchen, and the smell of freshly fried chicken permeated the air. Moving into the space, he saw his two brothers standing at the kitchen counter. The Stallion bloodline ran deep and there was no denying their kinship. They each had the same rugged good looks, their features chiseled and their eyes haunting. Their complexions were a warm caramel brown, each looking as if they belonged to each other.

"Howdy, big brother," Nicholas Stallion greeted.

Nathaniel Stallion waved a hand in Noah's direction.

"Hey, what are you two doing here?" he questioned. He dropped his keys, badge, and gun to the countertop.

The two men cut an eye at each other both shrugging their broad shoulders.

Noah looked from one to the other then shook his head. "And you're cooking. It must be serious!"

"It's not," Nicholas chimed.

"It is," Nathaniel quipped.

Noah shook his head. "Let me grab a shower and unwind before you two hit me with any bad news," he said as he turned in the direction of his bedroom.

"Dinner should be ready in thirty," Nicholas called out as he checked on the meat in the deep fryer.

As Noah made his exit, the two brothers started to bicker, their muffled voices echoing in the distance. He couldn't help but smile. When the duo had been younger, he would always have to intervene and mediate their disagreements. Despite their respective ages, some things never changed.

Some minutes later Noah felt like a new man. Showered and refreshed he moved back to his family room. The kitchen table was set for three, and Nick was filling oversized mason jars with ice and lemonade.

"Hey, do you remember Catherine Moore from high school?" Noah asked, interrupting the conversation the two men were having. "She was a cheerleader."

Both men paused, eyeing Noah then each other.

"She was the head cheerleader," Nathaniel said. "And she was dating some college frat boy, wasn't she?"

"She was a snob!" Nicholas interjected. "Her folks had money. Big money, and she wouldn't look in our direction if I remember correctly."

"You were a freshman. No one looked in your direction," Noah wisecracked.

Nathaniel laughed. "Didn't you have a crush on her? One of those hiding in the bushes, stalkerlike crushes?"

Noah rolled his eyes. "It wasn't that bad."

"Oh, yes, it was. She was popular and pretty and you had absolutely no game."

"He still doesn't," Nicholas said with a deep laugh.

Noah reached for the platter of cornbread, not bothering to respond.

"So, why are you asking about Catherine Moore?" Nicholas questioned, filling his own plate with string beans.

Noah shrugged. "No reason. I just ran into her today at my interview. She owns the company."

"That's right!" Nathaniel exclaimed. "How'd that go?"

"They offered me the job with a nice six-figure salary."

"Congratulations!" both brothers chimed in unison.

"Still not sure I'm going to take it, though."

"Why not?" Nicholas questioned.

Noah paused. The day after high school gradua-

tion he'd enlisted in the US Army. There had been
no money saved for him for college and he was determined to get a degree. Back then he saw the military as a means to an end. He'd given Uncle Sam
twelve years then had earned a bachelor's degree in
criminal justice. Joining the Salt Lake City police
department had been a natural progression and since
then he'd risen nicely through the ranks. He was now
the lead detective in the criminal investigations unit
and despite the gravity of some of his cases, he liked
what he did. He wasn't sure he was ready to let it go.

He didn't bother to answer his brother's question,
deciding to change the subject instead. "So, when are
you two going to tell me why you're here and not in
Los Angeles?"

Nicholas sighed. "It's really nothing."

"No, it's something," Nathaniel said. He turned
his gaze toward Noah. "Nicholas took a bad hit in the
game the other week and he bruised his back again.
He also damaged his knee."

"The one he fractured before?"

Nathaniel nodded. "At this point he needs to think
about his future. As his orthopedic specialist it's my
recommendation that he retire."

Nicholas pounded a fist against the table. "I'm not
retiring and I would appreciate it if you two didn't
talk about me like I wasn't in the room."

"If you continue to play football, you risk doing
some major damage that you're not going to be able
to come back from. Another hit like last week and

you may never walk again. That's your reality and I don't think you understand that," Nathaniel snapped.

Nicholas shrugged.

Nathaniel threw up his hands in frustration. "You need to talk to him," he said, turning his attention back to their older brother. "I can't get through to him."

Noah took a bite of his chicken and said nothing as his two younger siblings continued to squabble back and forth. He was almost finished with his meal when he finally offered a comment, quoting their late mother.

He shifted his gaze to look Nicholas in his eyes. "Live the ride," Noah said. "It's your life, and I can't tell you how to live it, but I can tell you to live it to the fullest. You only get to do this once. But with that said, you do need to consider your doctor's warning. Know the risks and heaven forbid if something happens, be willing to accept the consequences."

He turned to look at Nathaniel, who was shaking his head in disagreement. "Hey, you've told him everything he needs to know to make his decision. There's nothing else you can do except support him in whatever that is."

Nathaniel blew a heavy breath of air past his full lips. He shook his head.

Nicholas nodded then turned his attention to the television. A few minutes later he nodded his head at his brother. "So, you still want them season passes?"

Nathaniel met the look Nicholas was giving him. He hesitated only briefly before answering. "Hell, yeah!"

Noah smiled as a blanket of silence dropped over the trio. Across the big-screen television, New England was using Oakland to wipe the football field.

Hours later, Noah lay awake, his body sprawled atop his king-size mattress. Both his brothers had retired to guest rooms in his spacious home.

He was grateful for the bond they all shared. His family meant everything to him. Things had been slightly off when their baby sister, Natalie, had gone off to Europe, distancing herself from them, but all was well again. Natalie was back to being the prickly pain in his side that he adored.

He blew a heavy sigh, rolling onto his side as thoughts of Catherine Moore flashed through his mind. She was a beautiful woman, curvaceous with an incredible caramel-toned complexion. She also had a sharp wit and astute business acumen. He imagined some men were intimidated by her polished persona but there was no denying that her vivacious personality commanded attention the moment she entered a room. Noah had often imagined himself partnered with a woman like that. Building his career with the police department had put any inkling of a romantic relationship on the back burner. But Noah had always wanted his future to include a wife and children.

He suddenly wondered if a woman like Catherine ever thought about children. He reasoned that building a corporate empire had probably stalled any thoughts she might have had about a family. Something he remembered about her reminded him she might not be the kind of woman who wanted nannies and babysitters raising her children.

It had been one of those senior year parties, and everyone had gathered at Lindsey Gardens for a wiener roast and bonfire. One of the players from the basketball team had been stuck with his two younger siblings tagging along, and Catherine had stepped in to lend a helping hand. He'd eyed her most of that night, enamored with her gentle handling of the little boy and girl. It suddenly surprised him that he remembered that moment and he couldn't help but wonder why. Sleep came upon him suddenly as he fell into a deep slumber. His rest was sweet as thoughts of Catherine continued to trip through his dreams.

It was well after midnight, and Catherine was determined to be finished with the contract and financial documents that had held her attention since the day had started. She was preparing for a meeting with her executive team, planning to announce her intentions to take her company public. It was a decision that had been years in the making. Since the acquisition of her first luxury aircraft, Catherine debated whether or not to remain a private entity. With the shift in political climate and the state of the economy, she had known the day might come when the expansion of her business might mean offering the public stock in her company. Currently, the business was doing exceptionally well, Fly High an industry leader on top of their game. Her decision to go public was based more on being prepared for the future and not needing an infusion of cash to do what she wanted to do.

With the last document signed, she poured herself a glass of wine. As she took the first sip she remembered that it had been a minute since she'd last eaten. Her yogurt and granola breakfast had been her last meal. She finished off her glass of merlot before rising from her cushioned seat and moving to the kitchen pantry and then the refrigerator. With a box of table water crackers and a block of pepper jack cheese in hand she returned to her seat and poured herself a second glass of wine.

Her Manhattan penthouse was quiet. Nothing stirred. The only sounds echoing around the space were her heavy breathing and a ripple of paper as she flipped through one document after another.

Being alone had never bothered Catherine. She had always enjoyed solitude, no one else's noise intruding on her quiet. Alone had never been synonymous with lonely. She swallowed the last bit of her snack and followed it with another swig of the wine.

Business had always come first and being alone had been the consequence of that. She could barely recall her last official date let alone any relationship she'd been involved in. A coy smile suddenly pulled at her thin lips. She stared down to the lined paper she'd been jotting notes on. In three separate spots she'd written down Noah Stallion's name. She'd been intrigued seeing him again. He was no longer the scrawny kid she barely remembered. The man had presence, his stance strong and magnanimous. He was the sweetest eye candy, intelligent *and* good-looking. In their very brief encounter he had grabbed her attention and held it. Noah Stallion was the kind of man women longed for in their lives. Catherine was no exception.

She had breathed a sigh of relief when her friend Crystal had assured her no one in their circle of friends had dated the man.

"He didn't date anyone at Bountiful," Crystal had proclaimed. "Not one soul."

"I know he had to have dated someone in high school," Catherine had persisted.

"Nope. He worked part-time after school. He had brothers and sisters to help take care of. From what I remember about him he didn't have time to date. Hey, do you remember…"

Catherine had gotten lost in the reflections as the two women caught up on old times. Crystal's last question had brought her back to reality.

"So, do you plan to hire him or seduce him? Because I don't think you can do both."

With a deep sigh, she rose from her seat and headed to her bedroom. As she disrobed, slipping into a red silk nightie, she couldn't help but think about her life and the many difficult choices she'd made. Crystal was right. She couldn't do both. She couldn't become romantically involved with any employee of Fly High. She had signed Noah's formal offer of employment just hours earlier. With luck, Catherine thought, maybe he wouldn't take the job.

Chapter 3

Naomi Stallion laughed as Noah stood in front of the mirror trying on neckties. He was trying to determine which one would best complement the dark suit he was planning to wear to his high school reunion.

Noah narrowed his gaze as he turned to stare at her. "What's so funny?" he questioned.

"You are. Why are you wearing a suit? This is not another interview."

"No, it isn't, but I do want to dress to impress."

"Impress who?"

He shot her another look. "Why are you here?"

She shrugged her narrow shoulders. "What? I can't visit anymore?"

Noah rolled his eyes, tossing yet another tie aside. "Have you talked to Natalie?"

His sister nodded. "She and Tinjin are getting ready

for fashion week. He's introducing his new clothing line. She wants us all to fly to Paris to be there to support him."

"I'd like to go but if I take this new job it might not be doable for me."

"So what's stopping you from making a decision?"

"I like what I do and I'm good at it. I'm not sure I want to give that up."

Naomi nodded her understanding. "Did you talk to Nathaniel?"

"Yeah."

"He told you about Nicholas?"

"They were both here. They flew out this morning."

"Did you tell him that he needs to stop playing?"

"No, I didn't. I told him he needed to do whatever is in his heart."

"I'm sure that pissed Nathaniel off."

"Maybe, but it's not his decision to make."

A moment of silence swept between him and Naomi.

Naomi let out a soft sigh then changed the subject. "Are you ready for me to style you so that you can actually make it to the reunion? Because at the rate you're going you might make it to one five years from now."

Noah grinned. "I'm not doing well, am I?"

"You're making a hot mess of things is what you're doing."

Naomi rose from her seat on the bed and moved into his walk-in closet. Minutes later she exited with a pair of Diesel steel-gray denim jeans, a black-and-gray-striped knit sweater and his black leather blazer.

"This says you're accomplished but not boasting. It's casual, comfortably stylish and gives you just enough of a bad boy flair to get some attention. Pair it with your black Timberlands."

Noah nodded. "How do you do that?"

"You usually do it yourself when you're not over-thinking," she said as she began to rehang the neckties he'd tossed onto the bed. "So are you going to tell me why you're so squirrely about going to your reunion?"

He shrugged, trying unsuccessfully to maintain a neutral expression on his face.

Naomi laughed. "Enough said. For your sake I just hope she's worth it!"

Noah shook his head. "Get out of my room, please, I need to get dressed."

Naomi was still laughing as she moved toward the door. "I know her friend Crystal. Do you want me to put in a good word for you?"

"Excuse me?"

"With Catherine. Do you want me to put in a good word for you? The twins said you were asking about her."

Taking two good strides toward the entrance, Noah pushed his sister out and closed the door in her face. He could hear her laughing all the way back to the family room.

He shook his head. Of all his siblings, he was closest to Naomi. The twins were two years younger than he was but always had a unique bond that naturally came with sharing the womb with someone. He'd been six, almost seven when their baby sister, Natalie, had been born, and even then Noah was already filling that paternal role that none of them had ever had. It had been different with Naomi, her maternal instincts putting them on equal footing. He'd been protective but hadn't needed to shelter her. Naomi was fierce, having an indomitable spirit like no other. And from the moment she'd drawn breath Naomi had been able to read him like no one else. She sometimes knew what he was thinking before he could even form the thought in his own mind. That sixth sense of hers could sometimes drive him crazy.

Minutes later he stood in front of his full-length mirror, staring at his reflection. Once again Naomi had gotten it right. Moving out of the room he found his sister in his family room with her feet up on the coffee table and a large bowl of popcorn in her lap. An episode of some reality show was playing on his big screen. He stood watching for a brief moment as two young women spat insults at each other.

"Why do you watch this trash?" he questioned as he shifted his gaze back to his sister.

"Mindless television helps me unwind."

"Well, you got the mindless part right," he said, shaking his head as the two women on the screen began throwing punches.

"That's some rapper's girlfriend and his other girlfriend. Neither one knows he has a wife," Naomi said as she tossed a handful of kernels into her mouth.

Noah rolled his eyes. "Are you staying here tonight or are you going back to Norris Jean's house?" he said, referring to their late mother's home. The twelve-hundred-square-foot manufactured home had been empty since her passing. Although it had almost been a full year, he and his family were taking their time to decide what they wanted to do with the property.

Naomi shrugged. "I haven't decided yet. I finished cleaning out the spare bedroom earlier. I need to start working on her bedroom but I might wait until Natalie comes back so we can do it together. Do you mind if I stay here?"

Noah shook his head. "You know better than that. You know you're welcome here anytime."

"I had to ask. I didn't know if you were planning on bringing someone home from the reunion or not. You might have wanted to get your freak on in private."

Noah laughed as he grabbed his keys and wallet and headed for the door. "Good night, Naomi."

"Have fun, Noah. And you look good, by the way."

An oversized banner welcomed the Bountiful High School class back for their high school reunion. Pulling his SUV into a parking spot near the gymnasium door Noah sat watching as his former classmates streamed inside.

He recognized Brighton Laramie and August Thames, both former members of the football team who were both currently on probation. One had done time for a drug infraction, the other for domestic violence against his wife. Noah wasn't much interested in catching up with either.

Leslie Prentiss, the girl who'd graduated valedictorian, strolled hand in hand with a man he didn't recognize, but he fathomed the stranger was probably her husband. Everyone entering the building looked happy to be there and excited at the prospect of reconnecting with old friends.

As he was about to step out of his car, an oversized limo pulled up to the curb. Everyone around paused to watch the limo driver move around the front of the car to open the passenger side door. Noah smiled as he recognized the members of Bountiful's former cheerleading team: Brittney, Margie, Patricia, Valerie and the Three Cs—Crystal, Camille, and Catherine.

The years had been good to them, figures still tight, faces still pretty. Patricia's added weight gave her curves like she'd never had before, and Camille's very pregnant belly garnered much attention. The sight of them brought back a flood of memories, and Noah smiled.

The cheerleaders had teased and tormented him in high school. He'd been painfully shy around girls, and they'd found amusement in making him squirm. Even then he'd known that no one meant him any malice or harm but their frequent antics had made for many awkward moments. He watched as they all moved inside the building before stepping out of his car and following them inside.

The high school's gymnasium had been decorated for the occasion, reminding him of the one or two school dances he'd actually attended. Black and red crepe paper streamers and miniature white lights floated along the ceiling. There were large round tables covered in white tablecloths and large, red pillar candles and carnation arrangements sat as centerpieces. A nice crowd had already gathered, many laughing, smiling faces around the room.

Bridget Wilson sat at the reception table in the entrance collecting contact information and handing out name tags with people's high school images. The senior portraits were a reminder of a very different time in all of their lives.

Bridget waved excitedly in his direction. The two frequently crossed paths in their lines of work. Bridget was with the district attorney's office and often referred him to young men and boys who seemed wanting and willing to work their way out of the judicial system. Noah had mentored many of them successfully, their futures now more about college and success than the trappings of prison initially promised for their bad choices. The two had dated briefly but nothing had come of it, Bridget was now married to another attorney.

"Hey, Bridget. How are you?"

"I'm great, Noah. I'm so glad you came."

Noah nodded. "Naomi made me. She swore I'd regret it years from now if I didn't."

"Your sister is a wise woman."

"Where's Don?"

"That husband of mine refused to come. You know how anti-social he is."

Noah smiled and shrugged as she rose from her seat to tie a red band around his wrist.

"This gives you two drinks," she said, moving back to the other side of the table. "Is your email address still the same?"

"Yes, ma'am."

"Then you're good to go. Have yourself a good time."

Noah gave her a slight wave as he moved inside. The music was loud, a DJ playing all the hits from back in the day. Michael Jackson's "Rock with You" vibrated through the air, a few of the women dancing in front of the stage. As Noah headed for a seat at an empty table, he was stopped in his tracks.

Tyrone Bellamy, Christopher McDowell and Sean Parrish greeted him with brash handshakes and gregarious hugs.

"Noah Stallion!"

"Yo, dude! Is that you?"

"Noah!"

"It's good to see you guys," Noah chimed. "So what have y'all been up to?"

"I'm still working at my dad's hardware store," Sean said.

"I'm teaching here at the high school and coaching the boy's baseball team," Tyrone said.

Christopher nodded. "I left Salt Lake City. I'm in New York now working on Wall Street. What about you?"

"I'm working with the local police department," Noah answered.

"Any kids?" Christopher asked.

He shook his head. "No. No wife, no kids. You?"

"I've got two."

"I've got one on the way," Tyrone said, a wide grin across his face.

"Well, I've got six kids." Sean laughed.

"Six?" they all said in unison and turned to stare at the man.

He nodded. "Six kids, four baby mamas and three failed marriages, so no more wives or kids for me ever again."

Noah laughed as they all nodded their understanding.

A loud scream echoed from behind them. As Noah turned, a petite woman with a blonde bob and bright blue eyes flung herself against him. The trio he'd been chatting with waved goodbye and headed for the bar, leaving him to fend for himself.

"Noah Stallion! I'd know you anywhere!" she said excitedly. "How are you?"

"Marilyn Hodges. I'm good. How are you?"

"It's Marilyn Beeker now. I married Charlie Beeker."

"Charlie, who almost burned down the science lab senior year, Charlie?"

"That's the one." She giggled. "And he's still a pyro. He burned down my screened porch last year." She laughed as if there were something actually funny about that.

But Noah laughed with her. "Well, it's good to

see you," he said as he thought back to Mr. Milner's math class when she'd regularly cheat off his paper and he let her.

From the corner of his eye he spied Catherine sitting in conversation with two men. He recognized them but couldn't put a name to either face. He turned to stare blatantly. Marilyn seemed to read his mind.

"You remember Catherine Moore, don't you? She's CEO of some big business. I hear she's engaged to be married to some European art dealer. And that's Bo Wells and Mark Spencer. Bo's a photographer now, and I don't know what Mark is doing."

Noah nodded. "So she's engaged?"

"Yeah, but I told her marriage isn't all it's cracked up to be," she said with a deep chortle. "Not at all!"

Noah smiled as she gave him a quick hug and skipped off to catch up with someone else. He moved toward the bar, walking away with a bottle of chilled beer. Moving off to a corner, he sat alone, still watching everyone around him. Occasionally, a familiar face would stop to chat, catching him up on what they'd done with their lives since graduation. Many had married and had kids. A few were living very exotic lives, and then there had been the select few who still had no clue what they wanted to do with their lives. After a while the stories all began to sound alike.

Noah had come to the reunion hoping to see Catherine and maybe talk with her more. Hearing she was planning to be someone's wife had burst his bubble, and he was suddenly feeling deflated. He tipped the bottle of brew to his mouth and took a big sip.

He glanced down at his watch. It had been a good time and although it was still fairly early, he saw no reason to stay any longer. Moving back to his feet, he headed into the men's room before making his exit. Inside, two more acquaintances were telling the same lie, both trying to make what little they'd accomplished seem like so much more. Washing his hands with soap and water, Noah wished both men well.

He swiped his hands across a paper towel and headed for the door. Outside the men's room, he paused, staring down the school's hallway at the long line of lockers that ran the length of the wall. He could almost hear the youthful laughter that used to ring in the air back in the day and it made him smile.

Standing in the hallway, he moved to the glass case that housed the sports awards, admiring the many trophies and mementos the athletic department had amassed over the years. He stopped to reflect on an image of him and the team taken at their senior class sport's dinner. That time felt like an eternity ago.

With a deep sigh, he turned abruptly, heading in the direction of the door. As he did, he just missed slamming into Catherine Moore, once again avoiding a potential catastrophe.

She laughed warmly, her voice low and seductive. "You saved me again, Noah Stallion!"

Noah's smile widened. "It does look that way, Catherine."

"Please, call me Cat. Only strangers call me Catherine."

"You look beautiful tonight, Cat," he said as his gaze skated the length of her body.

She wore a knee-length skirt with a yoked waist with tightly pulled gathered material and a full ruffled petticoat beneath it. The color was dark granite partnered with a tailored white blouse and platform pumps in a bright floral pattern on a black background. Her look was stylish and sexy.

She smiled. "Thank you." She narrowed her gaze on his face. "You're not leaving, are you?"

He nodded. "I think I've had my fill of memory lane trips for tonight."

She nodded but said nothing as she stood staring at him. There was a heated wave of energy that surged between them. Her gaze was intoxicating, and Noah felt his body reacting. He took a deep breath and held it for a brief moment before letting it out slowly.

"I'm actually headed back to the hotel myself," she said. "Why don't you join me? We can grab a drink in the hotel's bar and catch up without all the noise."

Noah's gaze was still connected with hers. He suddenly felt like a snake being charmed. He nodded, completely possessed. "I'd like that. I'd like that a lot."

Catherine smiled. "The girls are riding home in the limo. I'll grab my purse. We can take your car, if you don't mind." Her tone was commanding as she turned on her high heels and disappeared back into the gym.

* * *

Camille and Crystal tossed each other a look as Catherine rushed back toward the table.

"Where are you going?" Camille questioned as Catherine grabbed her leather handbag and guzzled down the last of her drink.

"Back to the hotel."

Crystal looked toward the entrance where Noah Stallion stood staring in their direction. "Are you going alone?" she asked, her expression all knowing.

Catherine grinned. "Not that it's any of your business, but no, I'm not."

Her two friends both shook their heads, amusement painting their expressions.

"It's about time," Crystal said. "I was starting to think that all you two were going to do was stare at each other all night long."

Camille nodded in agreement. "I can't believe he's still that shy. Are you sure something's not wrong with him? I mean, you have been known to date really good-looking men that have actually turned out to be complete freaks. Wasn't one of your exes a serial killer?"

"He's not that shy and he's not a freak," Catherine answered, "and you know darn well I have never dated a serial killer." She leaned to hug and kiss one and then the other. "I'll call you later."

"I know I don't need to give you my 'practice safe sex' speech, right?" Crystal asked as she hugged her friend back.

Catherine laughed. "I think I've got this handled."

Camille laughed. "Girl, bye! Just go have fun!"

Tossing them both one last smile, Catherine headed toward Noah, her excitement practically beating her to his side.

Chapter 4

Minutes later, they were careening down Poplar Grove Boulevard, just six miles from the Hotel Monaco. Catherine had rolled down the window, allowing the cool evening breeze to blow through her hair, the highlighted strands falling past her shoulders. There was a comfortable level of quiet that had settled over them, and neither spoke—no words were needed as they acclimated themselves to the emotion building between them. And something was building, the thickness of it completely intoxicating.

As they waited at a stoplight, she turned toward Noah, the streetlight illuminating her face. There was a halo of sparkle around her head, and Noah thought she had to be the most exquisite female he'd ever known. They both smiled again as they caught each other's gaze.

"So how long are you in town?" Noah finally asked, breaking the silence.

She shrugged her narrow shoulders. "I'm only here for the weekend. I have to be in Atlanta next week then back in New York."

"You get around."

She chuckled softly. "I do," she said as she shifted her gaze back out the window.

"Is that a good thing?"

She shrugged again. "I never thought about it."

"How does your fiancé feel about it?"

Her head snapped back in his direction. Her eyebrows lifted in amusement. "My fiancé? What fiancé?"

Noah's eyes skated in her direction then back to the road. "Someone at the reunion said you were engaged to an artist or something."

Catherine laughed. The sound was musical, a warm treble that filled the air between them. "I bet it was Crystal or Camille that told that lie. I am not engaged, nor have I ever been married. I don't even have a steady boyfriend."

Noah grinned. "Oh," he said. "Sorry to hear that."

"Are you really?"

He shook his head. "No."

She laughed again, and he laughed with her.

As he pulled into a parking spot in front of the hotel they kept eyeing each other, grinning foolishly. Noah felt like he was seventeen all over again. Moving into the lobby, Catherine led the way toward the hotel bar. Grabbing his hand she pulled him along to a cushioned seat in the corner, gesturing for the bartender as she reluctantly released the hold she had on his fingers. They sat down, facing each other, their bodies close as they shared the seat.

"What's your poison?" Catherine asked as she shifted forward in her seat.

"I'll take a beer. Corona with a twist of lime."

"I'll have a glass of white wine," she said to the young man who'd come to take their orders.

She sat back as she rested her arm atop the seat's back and leaned her head on her hand. She lifted her leg so that her knee was lightly pressed against the side of his upper thigh. Her touch was heated, and Noah felt himself break out into a sweat.

She lifted her eyes to stare at him. "So tell me what you've been doing since we graduated, Noah Stallion."

Noah chuckled. "Do you want me to recap the highlights of my résumé or give you the whole spiel?"

"I don't want your résumé. I know what you've accomplished in your professional life, remember? I want to hear about your personal life. I want to know if the guy voted best personality and most likely to marry a supermodel ever did."

His head moved from side to side, a slight blush warming his complexion as he laughed. He ran a hand over his freshly shaven head. The gesture drew her attention, and Catherine stared.

Noah Stallion had grown into himself. Gone was

that baby-faced high-school student. His chiseled features had matured nicely. His eyes were dark pools, his nose almost too perfect and he had the most luscious lips of any man Catherine had ever known. They were full, like thick pillows, and she couldn't help but wonder what they would feel like pressed against hers. She heard herself gasp out loud, suddenly embarrassed that she'd been staring so wantonly.

"What is it?" Noah asked, meeting the look she was giving him.

She shook her head, desperate to suddenly shake the rise of emotion from her. "Nothing. I was just waiting to hear about you."

"You were staring."

"I was."

"Why were you staring at me?"

She blinked as he eyed her curiously. "Get over it, please. I did it, it was rude, but I'm not going to explain it or apologize for it."

Their gazes held, and then Noah laughed again.

His deep chortle moved her to giggle. He suddenly reached out his hand to brush a lock of hair from her face. His touch was gentle and easy, like a cool breeze on a summer night. Catherine felt a tingle of heat waft through her, moving her to hold her breath.

Noah finally answered her question. "There's really nothing to tell. I've been focused on my career. And no, I never married. I have no children and no drama in my life other than things my siblings manage to get themselves into. And now, here we are."

She nodded. "Here we are."

Noah took his own deep breath. "So tell me about you. About your personal life when you weren't building a multi-million-dollar empire."

"Doing that didn't leave me much time for anything else." She let out a low sigh.

"Do you regret it?" Noah asked, noting the expression that crossed her face.

She shook her head. "Not at all. I still have time. It's not like I'm that old."

"That's true."

"Do you regret not having a family yet?"

Noah pondered the question. He'd never really given it any thought. He'd been taking care of people since he'd been a boy. Truth be told it was really all he knew. Being the oldest, he'd always been responsible for his younger brothers and sisters. He'd stepped in to do what their wayward father had refused to do and what his mother hadn't been able to do by her lonesome. He didn't miss not having kids because he felt like he'd already raised four of them. But he did miss companionship and having a partner by his side to share his life with.

He met the curious look she was giving him. "I guess *regret* is not the right word. I wish things were different but the right woman just never came along."

"Until now?" Catherine's eyes were wide, her brazen remark surprising them both.

He laughed, his gaze narrowing slightly. "You never know."

Her smile was wide and bright, warming his spirit.

"Noah Stallion, I do believe you are blushing!" she exclaimed, trying to deflect the attention back on him.

"I'm sure I am. I'm not use to a woman putting me on the spot like that."

"Oh, yes, you are. I'm sure women put you on the spot all the time."

"Why would you say that?"

"Because you're an easy target. I don't think you realize…" She paused, biting down against her bottom lip as she searched for the right words to explain herself.

"Realize what?" Noah persisted.

"I don't think you realize the power you have with women. You're the whole package. You're intelligent, good-looking, well-rounded, good-looking, kind, good-looking…"

Noah laughed, a wave of embarrassment flushing his face. "I got the good-looking."

"And that's my point. You don't see what women do so you're not full of yourself or arrogant, and that makes you even more desirable. I bet half the time you don't even know when women are hitting on you."

He nodded. "You're right. I don't."

"Which leaves you blushing a lot, I'm sure."

"So, are you hitting on me?" His expression was just shy of smug.

She smiled, meeting his gaze evenly, but she didn't respond. Instead, she took a slow sip of her drink. The look she gave him made Noah laugh heartily. She changed the subject.

"I was sorry to hear about your mother passing," she said, her tone soft.

"Thank you." Their gazes locked for a moment before Noah dropped his eyes to the space of sofa between them.

"Is your father still living?"

Noah shrugged his broad shoulders. "He is, but we never knew our father. You might know him, though. Nolan Perry?"

Her eyes widened. "Reverend Perry is your father?"

Noah nodded. "The one and only. My mother followed him here to Utah from Texas when she was fifteen. He was the love of her life but he abandoned her and never had anything to do with us kids."

She pressed a hand against his arm as he continued.

"I went to see him once but he wouldn't even speak to me."

"I'm so sorry. You didn't deserve that."

He shrugged again. "It is what it is. I don't think about it much anymore."

A look of sadness flashed in his eyes, and Catherine sensed that wasn't quite true.

"You came from a big family, didn't you? You had a lot of brothers and sisters, right?"

"Two brothers and two sisters. My brother Nicholas plays football for Los Angeles and his twin, Nathaniel, is an orthopedic surgeon."

Catherine nodded. "I remember the twins."

"And then there's my sister Naomi. She's a holistic life coach, and my baby sister, Natalie, is a high-fashion model."

"I don't remember Natalie but I know Naomi. She and Crystal are good friends. Crystal uses a ton of her hair care products."

"Naomi's actually built a very successful organic health care business. I'm very proud of her."

"I don't remember you guys socializing much while we were in school."

Noah shrugged. "We couldn't afford it. Besides, you and your click weren't interested in hanging out with us poor kids."

"That's not true. I remember we spent a lot of time together after football practice and at the games."

Noah laughed. "I remember you used to give me a hard time."

She grinned. "See, I was even hitting on you back then and you didn't have a clue."

Noah thought back to the times they'd spent together. Catherine and her friends hadn't cut him any slack. The teasing had been formidable. A slow smile pulled at his mouth. Back then, Noah didn't say much but he didn't run from situations, either. Having the cheerleaders hanging on him had, in some ways, been a badge of honor, giving him favor among his peers. But what he remembered most about that time was that it had taken little for them to leave him hard and wanting. Back then a warm breeze would leave his teenaged body with an erection. Catherine Moore and the cheerleading squad were a warm breeze times ten. He laughed out loud, and Catherine laughed with him.

Before either realized it, they'd been talking for almost two hours. It was almost midnight, the bar had closed and they were still sitting together in the hotel's lobby, completely enamored with each other. Noah had never told anyone as much about his childhood as he found himself sharing with Catherine. They talked about his family, her parents, their dreams and their fears. They had more in common than not and they made each other laugh. Their conversation was comfortable and easy and Noah imagined that it could have lasted forever without any effort.

"So, what made you want to leave your job?" Catherine asked. "You sound like you really enjoy what you do."

"I actually haven't made a decision. I was very flattered that your organization was interested in me but I'm not sure if that's what I really want for myself."

"So there's still a chance that you might not work for Fly High?"

"There is."

She pondered his statement for a moment. Crystal's comment days before suddenly popped into her thoughts. She had never before given any consideration to pursuing a relationship with a Fly High employee. But technically, Noah didn't work for her, and might not ever.

Noah stared intently as she drifted off into thought,

his gaze skating over her face as he inhaled her features. Catherine Moore was incredibly beautiful. Her complexion was a warm coffee with much cream and her features were fine and delicate. There was an air of fragility about her, her cover-model looks belying her authoritative personality. It was her strength that he found most attractive. Everything about her moved him like no other woman before her. He found the sensation only slightly unnerving.

She suddenly stood up, turning to stare down at him. A wave of anxiety flitted across her face as she looked him in the eye. "So, either this is going to be a monumental mistake or it's not." She took a deep breath and then another, blowing the air out in a loud gust. "I think we have great chemistry, Noah Stallion. And since you don't work for me yet and I think you and I could be very good together, would you like to come up to my room?" Her hands were clenched in tight fists at her sides, her nervousness blanketing her posture. "And please don't think this is something I do often, because it's not," she said, suddenly feeling like she needed to explain herself. "You're the first man I've ever invited back to my hotel room like this."

Noah moved onto his feet beside her. He stepped in close, and she gasped, the nearness of him so intense that it drew the oxygen from her lungs. When he eased an arm around her slim waist and pulled her even closer, she thought she might faint. She grabbed the front of his leather jacket to steady herself, her hands grazing his chest.

"What's going to happen if I do take the job?" he questioned, his voice dropping to a loud whisper. "If we do this, then how…" His voice trailed.

She took another deep breath. Her eyes darted back and forth, purposely trying to avoid his. "We're both adults. If you do decide to take the job I think we can be mature about the whole thing. I just know that…well…I just know what I'm feeling right now."

"And what's that? What are you feeling?"

She finally lifted her eyes to his, falling headfirst into the stare he was giving her. In that moment everything in her head became a muddled mess. Seconds earlier it had all made sense, now it didn't.

"I… Well…we…" she stammered. Her face was flushed, heat tinting her cheeks a brilliant shade of red.

Noah puller her even closer. Both his hands snaked from the curve of her waist to around her back. She felt amazing in his arms, like she'd been born to be there. He dropped his head slightly, his mouth just millimeters away from hers. His warm breath was teasing and her own lips parted in anticipation. Noah hesitated as he pressed his forehead to hers. Her perfume was light, an airy floral scent that tickled his nostrils. He brushed his cheek against her cheek as he wrapped his arms tightly around her torso, hugging her easily. He whispered, the warmth of his words blowing past her earlobe. "I feel the same way," he said.

They held hands as they rode the elevator to the sixth floor, shooting each other anxious looks. Noah

followed her down the hallway to her room door.
Once inside, the door closed and locked behind them,
Noah felt his anxiety rising swiftly. The comfort he'd
initially found with Catherine was nowhere to be
found. An anxious chill shot through his body and
it concerned him. He was suddenly self-conscious,
second guessing his current situation.

Catherine seemed to read his mind. "If you relax,
I'll relax," she said. She stood in the center of her
room, her eyes wide and her body quivering slightly.

He smiled. "I'm relaxed."

She laughed. "You don't look relaxed and you
definitely don't sound too convincing."

"Really," he said, his head bobbing up and down.
"I'm very relaxed."

Catherine rolled her eyes. "How many women
have you slept with, Noah?"

Surprise pierced his stare. "Excuse me?"

"How many women…"

"I heard the question the first time."

She crossed her arms over her chest. "Well?"

"Not nearly as many as you probably think," he
answered, a smile pulling at his full lips. "How many
have you slept with?"

She shrugged. "None. I don't sleep with women."

Noah chuckled. "Very funny, but I guess I walked
right into that."

Catherine grinned. "Now you look relaxed."

She kicked off her high heels as she crossed the
room to turn on the sound system. A Sam Smith song
played. The tune was soulful and sexy.

Noah watched as she stood with her eyes closed, taking it in. He moved farther into the room, closer to the king-size bed that occupied most of the floor space. Catherine moved to his side, brushing a manicured hand across his back.

"Excuse me a minute while I freshen up," she said. Their gazes locked for just a brief second before she turned away. She headed into the adjoining bathroom, closing the door between them.

Noah let out an anxious sigh. He couldn't remember the last time he'd been so nervous, despite his best efforts not to let it show. But he was anxious and excited. He dropped down onto the corner of the bed then stood back up abruptly. He moved to the window, peeking past the drapes out to the parking lot below. He eased back to the bed, changed his mind for a second time and then moved to sit on the sofa. He sat down, resting his forearms against his thighs, clasping his hands tightly together in front of his face. Feeling awkward he shifted back against the seat cushions, crossing one leg over the other. Time seemed to tick slowly as he suddenly jumped back up. He took off his leather jacket and sat back down. He let out another deep sigh, dismayed by his own behavior. Frustration creased his brow. He had never been this nervous with any other woman, not even that first time when he'd lost his virginity.

Catherine suddenly stuck her head out the bathroom. Just as she did there was a knock on the exterior door. "That's room service," she said. "Can you get that while I take a quick shower?"

"No problem," Noah said as he jumped to his feet and crossed the room in four quick strides.

"Good evening, sir," the young man standing on the other side of the door greeted him. He rolled in a cart laden with silver covered trays. He turned to pass the order ticket to Noah.

"Thanks, buddy," Noah said as he reached into his pocket for a tip. He pulled a ten-dollar bill into his hands and passed it to the guy.

After the door was closed and locked behind the man he moved to inspect what had been left on the trays. "What did you order?" he yelled as he lifted the silver lids from their platters.

There were bowls of freshly popped popcorn, slices of cake, two burgers, a pasta salad dish, a liter of soda and bottles of water.

Minutes later, Catherine exited out of the bathroom. She'd changed out of her clothes and was wearing a pair of flannel pajamas. Her hair was pulled up in a loose ponytail. She'd washed the makeup from her face and she looked relaxed and comfortable.

"Cute," he said, smiling at her.

"Thank you."

"I thought you might be hungry," she said as she grabbed one of the burgers and a bowl of popcorn and moved to the bed, crawling toward the headboard. "I know I'm famished and food always relaxes me." She turned off the sound system and turned on the television.

Noah laughed as he caught the look she tossed him. Kicking off his own shoes, he grabbed the other meal. Side by side they enjoyed the late-night snack as they watched the latest Denzel Washington movie on the hotel's pay-per-view station. When they were done eating and the dishes were cleared away, Catherine leaned into his side, resting her head on his shoulder. Every so often Noah would trail his hand across her arm or the back of her hand, his touch teasing. As the movie credits ran, he threw his legs off the side of bed and stood up.

Catherine eyed him anxiously. "Is everything okay?"

"Yes." He nodded. "I'm just going to use the bathroom."

She smiled as he disappeared into the other room. When the door was closed behind him she sank into the pillows, pulling one up and over her head. Feeling out of sorts, Catherine couldn't begin to put her feelings into words. She'd invited Noah back to the hotel thinking that all she wanted was a night of wild, passionate, unencumbered sex. It felt like it had been forever since she'd met a man she wanted to be with. In the back of her mind, they could have made love to each other without either wanting or needing more. But with each passing moment she was beginning to realize that a one-night stand wasn't really what she was looking for at all.

From the other room she could hear the sound of water running, and she realized Noah was taking a shower. She stood up, moving her body off the bed. She began to pace anxiously, suddenly realizing that she did want more. She wanted a man just like Noah

Stallion in her life. And she wanted him for longer than a few passion-filled hours. The prospect of exploring where the two of them could possibly take that had her even more excited.

Her grandmother would have said that Noah Stallion was a man worth twice his weight in gold. There was something about him that had her rethinking everything she'd ever believed about men and relationships and how both could fit into the dynamics of her life. And as the sound of water stopped, the prospect of seeing him naked, his skin heated and damp from the steam, suddenly had her salivating, her heart beating with a vengeance in her chest. She couldn't begin to know what to do with all that emotion. Everything she was feeling scared her to death.

Chapter 5

Noah passed a plush white towel across his skin, swiping at the water that saturated the surface. He had needed a cold shower to stall the rise of desire that was sweeping between him and Catherine. He hadn't known what to expect when she'd invited him to her room but what he hadn't anticipated was feeling as connected to her as he did. They were having an amazing time with each other. She was fun, and he felt completely at ease in her presence. And he wanted her, the intensity of his desire was consuming. But she wasn't looking for forever and he didn't know exactly what he was looking for. It was confusing, and a wealth of emotion was clouding the situation.

In all his years, he couldn't remember ever feeling

so unsure of himself or his feelings. But he was sure of one thing. He wanted her. He wanted her like he had never wanted any other woman. And if he were honest with himself, he had wanted her since they'd been seventeen years old when she used to give him grief after football practice. But under their current circumstances he didn't have a clue where that would leave the two of them when all was said and done.

He took a deep breath as he wrapped a towel around his waist. Suddenly, he knew that making love to Catherine and walking away wasn't fathomable. He could never walk away from her and all they had done thus far was lay the foundation for a beautiful lifelong friendship.

Minutes later when Noah stepped out of the bathroom he was fully dressed. Catherine stood in the center of the room, her arms wrapped tightly around her torso.

"I think we should call it a night," Catherine quickly said.

"Yeah, I really should be going," he said almost before she could finish her statement.

There was a sudden awkward silence that swelled thick and full between them. Catherine was biting down on her bottom lip, nervous tension pulling her mouth into a frown.

She shook her head. "You must think I'm a crazy woman," she said, her voice a loud whisper.

"No. What I think is that I want to make love to you. And I think you want to make love to me. And if we make love I think we both know that it's not going to be a casual encounter that either of us is just going to forget about. So we need to regroup. That's what I think."

His comment struck a nerve, and she nodded, tears misting her gaze. "I should probably warn you that I've never done well with relationships," Catherine said.

Noah smiled. "Well, there's a first time for everything."

She smiled back. "I really had a great time tonight."

"So did I." He moved to her side and grabbed her hand, entwining their fingers together. "Walk me to the door," he said as he turned in the direction of the exit.

Catherine followed behind him, her other hand pressed against his lower back. Standing in the entranceway, Noah turned to face her. His eyes danced over her face. Leaning forward, he pressed a damp kiss to her cheek, his lips lingering. His touch ignited a raging flame deep in her core.

Pulling back, he lost himself in her eyes. Her stare was intoxicating. He pressed his hand to the side of her face, his fingers trailing the line of her profile. She leaned into his palm, closing her eyes as she relished the intensity of his touch. And then he kissed her. "You take my breath away, Cat Moore," he said as he met her gaze. He gave her one last peck on the lips then he turned, heading down the hallway.

Catherine stood staring after him. When he turned the corner, disappearing from sight, she began to shake. Her heartbeat was racing, and her eyes darted back and forth anxiously. The emotion was combustible. This was not how their night was supposed to end. She didn't want him to leave. She suddenly raced down the hall behind him.

Noah was standing in front of the bank of elevators. The conveyor door had just opened when Catherine rounded the corner. She called his name just as he stepped inside. He thrust his hand and arm between the closing doors to keep them open. Stepping back out of the conveyor, he embraced her as she threw her body against his, wrapping her arms around his neck. He held her tightly, nuzzling his face into her neck.

"Stay," Catherine said, lifting her eyes to his. "Please."

Noah stared intently, his gaze questioning.

Reading his mind she nodded. "I've never been more certain of anything else in my whole life."

There was nothing shy or quiet about Noah Stallion between the sheets. The man was dominating and powerful, and Catherine had absolutely no control, something that was completely foreign to her. But once the door had been locked behind them, Noah had taken command and she'd followed willingly.

He was playing her body like a master musician, knowing every key to strike, every note to play. Noah was successfully eliciting the most beautiful music from her, the sensations sweeping. Every one of her nerve endings was on fire, her interior combustible as his body danced in sync with hers.

Catherine clung to him, her long legs wrapped easily around his broad backside. Her hands skated across his back and shoulders as he pressed himself into her. Every stroke was slow and deliberate and teasing. Catherine felt as though he'd pierced her core, his touch soul deep. No one had ever reached her so intensely. Loving Noah was like nothing she'd ever experienced before.

His hands kneaded and caressed every square inch of her flesh until she was a quivering mess. He pushed and pulled himself in and out, their intimate connection a beautiful give and take. The sensations sweeping between them grew to a rousing crescendo sending them both spiraling off the edge of ecstasy at the same time.

Noah collapsed against her, panting heavily. Beneath him, Catherine gasped, fighting to catch her own breath. The moment had been telling—nothing about their encounter was what she had imagined. They clung to each other. She held him tightly as if she were afraid to let go. With a deep inhale, Noah rolled onto his side, pulling her closer against him.

Grabbing his hand, Catherine drew it to her lips and pressed a kiss against his palm. She kissed him a second time before folding his fingers into a fist as she closed her eyes.

Noah smiled and drifted off to sleep with her, his hand clutched to her heart.

As daylight seeped through the window, Noah lay flat against the mattress, his naked body sprawled beneath a white sheet. Still drifting between a state of slumber and wakefulness, he wasn't sure where he was or whose bed he was in. But then the memories came flooding back to him. Every sweet, decadent minute of his night with Catherine like a dream come true. He'd slept well and his dreams had been sweet. He didn't have one regret, their time together everything he had hoped it would be.

Beside him he felt Catherine's body shift onto the mattress top. He turned his head, opening his eyes. She sat cross-legged, staring down at him as she sipped on a cup of black coffee. He couldn't help but smile. She looked absolutely radiant.

"Good morning," Catherine chimed sweetly.

Noah rolled his body over so that he was now facing her. "Good morning."

"There's fresh coffee. Would you like a cup?"

He shook his head against a pillow. "No. Thank you. I don't drink coffee."

Catherine paused midsip. Her expression was incredulous. "What do you mean you don't drink coffee?"

"I don't. I don't like the taste."

"That's a problem for us already. I can't be with a man who doesn't drink coffee."

"Why not?"

"I just can't. What's going to happen when I come to your house and you don't have a coffeepot? It just won't work. I have to have my daily infusion."

He laughed. "I have a coffeepot, Cat. You'll be

fine. You'll be able to feed your addiction with no problems. I will even brew a fresh pot for you."

"You would do that for me?"

He trailed his thick fingers across her leg. "Only for you."

Catherine finished the sip she'd started. "Do you have any other weird dislikes for beverages or foods I need to know about?"

"No. Do you have any other deal breakers I should know about?"

She paused before answering. "Give me some time. I'm sure I can come up with something."

Noah shook his head. Rolling in the opposite direction, he threw his body off the side of the bed, moving onto his feet. He palmed his manhood as he moved into the bathroom, his naked backside waving in the new day.

"I left a new toothbrush on the counter for you," Catherine called after him, smiling as she watched him sway into the other room.

Minutes later Noah returned to the bed, his pearl-white teeth brushed and flossed, his face washed, his bladder empty. He leaned down to kiss her mouth. She tasted like coffee, sugar and minty toothpaste.

Catherine pressed her palm to his cheek. She loved kissing Noah. Loved how his mouth fit so perfectly against hers. How swiftly his tongue tangled with her tongue. His taste and scent were the sweetest delicacy. In the past twelve hours they'd kissed a lot. And she looked forward to that never stopping anytime soon.

"Do you have plans?" Catherine asked as Noah settled back down against the mattress. "For today, I mean."

"I was going to spend the day with you, unless there was something else you had to do." His gaze was narrowed, the look he gave her taunting.

A wave of heat suddenly washed over her entire body. She grinned, her expression eager. "No. I was hoping to spend the day with you, too."

He nodded as he reached for her cup of coffee, taking it from her hands. He turned and placed it on the nightstand. Rolling back toward her, he bent his index finger and gestured for her to come to him. The hint of a smile pulled at her lips as she leaned into him, excited to follow wherever he planned to take her.

Noah pulled her into his arms and kissed her again. His hands rested against her hips then moved beneath the thin material of her tank top. He began to slowly massage one breast and then the other. Her lips parted as Noah's tongue pressed between them. Catherine eagerly accepted it, letting it probe and explore as she closed her eyes, losing herself as his hands teased and felt her up.

He slid one hand down between her legs and into the boy-cut panties she wore. She was slick to the touch, the thin material of her underwear soaked with her arousal. He hummed as his kiss deepened, his mouth racing against hers.

His fingers slid across her pubis, the pad of his index finger rubbing circles around her clit. When he sank his hand inside the deep gash, massaging her inner walls slowly, a spark of electricity ignited throughout her body.

She felt the hardness of his member rubbing against her as he pulled her body next to his. She reached down to the girth hanging between his legs, her whole hand wrapping around his magnificence. The heat from her touch made him moan. She began to stroke him slowly over and over again. With each pass of her palm she felt him harden more and more.

Noah then kissed and licked his way down her breasts, suckling on her with his lips and trapping each chocolate nipple between his teeth. He took complete control of her body.

Reaching across to the nightstand, he pulled a condom from a newly opened box and sheathed himself quickly. Rolling above her, Noah pushed her legs apart. Catherine allowed him to spread her thighs wide, knowing, waiting, ready to accept what was coming. She took a deep breath, the anticipation consuming. When he entered her, the intensity of his possession was overwhelming.

His strokes were long and deep as he pulled out and pushed in slowly. His pace intensified as he began to speed up moderately, then faster. Her whole body burned, waves of heat shooting from her feminine spirit. He gripped her buttocks with both hands, plowing into her.

Catherine wrapped her arms around his neck and her legs around his waist, holding tightly as he pumped inside of her over and over again. She felt her inner lining convulse around him, pulsing with a vengeance as the blood boiled through her veins. She suddenly climaxed and before she could catch her breath a second orgasm swept through her body. When Noah finally had his own orgasm, she'd lost count of the number of times he'd taken her to the edge of ecstasy only to pull her back and do it all over again.

When the alarm on Cat's cell phone sounded Monday morning, she reluctantly opened her eyes. She and Noah had existed in a state of mindless bliss for more than forty-eight hours and she wasn't ready for it to end.

Extending her arm across the bed, she expected to find Noah lying next to her, but he wasn't present. She jumped abruptly, rolling against the mattress as she looked around the room. Noah stood in front of the dresser and mirror pulling on his clothes. She lifted herself up on her elbows to stare at him.

Noah tossed her an easy smile. "Good morning."

"What's so good about it," she said, feigning an exaggerated pout. "Our mini vacation is over. Now we have to go back to our real lives."

Noah nodded. "We do, but that doesn't mean you and I have to be over. Unless you want us to be."

He turned, staring at her. Her hair was tousled atop her head. Sleep still teased her eyes, and her skin was flushed from the heat in the room. The sheets were pulled up to her waist and her breasts were exposed, her nipples standing at full attention. She looked beautiful as always.

"Have you ever had a long-distance relationship before?" she asked. She pulled her knees to her chest.

Noah shook his head. "No. Have you?"

"I've never been able to do a relationship in my own backyard, so long distance never stood a chance."

"So where does that leave us, Cat?" Noah moved from the mirror to the bedside, taking a seat beside her.

Their gazes locked, his stare intense.

"I like *us*, Noah. I really like us a lot."

Noah smiled. "Then we'll work it out." He leaned to kiss her cheek. "Right now, though, I have to run. I need to stop home before I head to the station. I'll call you later today. We can talk then about what we're going to do next."

She nodded, reaching her arms upward to wrap around his neck. She hugged him tightly, her bare breasts pressed against his silk T-shirt, her face nestled against his chest. He hugged her back, holding her tight. Both inhaled simultaneously. She took in deep breaths of his scent, wanting to hold on to the sweet aroma she's quickly grown to adore.

Noah kissed the top of her head, her forehead, her cheek, before kissing her mouth one more time. "Have a safe flight," he said as he stood back up. He reached for his jacket and slipped it on.

Catherine nodded. "Thank you," she said. "This was the best weekend I've had since forever."

Noah winked at her. He smiled, then without another word he was gone.

Sliding off the bed, Catherine rushed to the door, peering out as he sauntered down the hallway. When Noah had disappeared around the corner she shut the door, securing it tightly. Tears pressed hot behind her eyelids. For reasons she didn't understand, she felt like crying. It took everything she had not to blubber like a baby. She wrapped her arms around her torso and hugged herself tightly.

She missed Noah already, feeling like she'd lost a piece of herself. Missing him hurt, and she didn't know how she would handle that kind of pain.

Moving back to the bed, Catherine crawled between the covers, pulling the sheets up over her head. The entire weekend with Noah had been one learning experience after another. Catherine had discovered much about herself in the short period of time they'd spent together.

She had enjoyed not thinking about business for a moment, something she hadn't done since starting her own business fifteen years ago. She liked the way Noah challenged her to rethink ideas she'd once been certain of, concepts she never questioned. He was intelligent and pragmatic and he had a keen sense of humor.

Noah made her laugh, laughed at her jokes and found the things she laughed at funny, as well. They'd debated politics, science, cartoons and theology. There was no topic they hadn't touched upon and she still had a long list of things she wanted to

discuss, interested in his opinion. She was anxious
for another opportunity to spend time with him.

She let out a deep sigh as she thought about him
and their time together. The sex! Oh, the sex! Catherine clenched her knees tightly together to stall the
quiver of heat between her legs that abruptly craved
attention. Noah had taken her to new heights. He'd
been gentle and attentive to her needs, but also dom-
ineering and possessive. He'd loved her with every
square inch of his body, and it had been the most
beautiful experience that had her craving for more.
Catherine had never wanted for anything the way
she was suddenly wanting Noah.

She tossed aside the covers, grabbing her phone
to check the time. Minutes later she stood beneath
a cold shower, willing the icy flow to cool the heat
that raged over her body. She knew what she was
feeling wouldn't last forever. In less than an hour
she would be back on one of her planes headed to
the east coast. By the evening it would be business
as usual and the weekend would be nothing but a
sweet, sweet memory.

Chapter 6

When Noah arrived home, Naomi was blending fruit and vegetables in his premium blender. She came to an abrupt stop as he entered the room.

"Hey," he said, tossing her a look.

"Really?"

"What?"

"You've been gone all weekend and all you can say is *hey*?"

"I sent you a text message that I wouldn't be home."

"That was two days ago! I figured that meant you weren't coming home Friday night, not that you'd be gone the entire weekend."

"Did you miss me, little sister?"

"No."

"Then it's all good."

Naomi shook her head, rolling her eyes before she turned back to the blender. "Do you want a smoothie?"

Noah headed toward his bedroom. "Yes, please."

Behind the closed door, he stripped out of his clothes and headed for a hot shower. Beneath the spray of warm water, he tilted his head, savoring the moist sensation against his skin. He was tense, every sinewy muscle in his body taut. His nerves were on edge and had been since he'd woken.

Being with Catherine had been a dream come true. The time they'd spent together from the moment they'd escaped the reunion until he'd left her hotel room exceeded all of his expectations.

Catherine made his heart sing. She was funny and snarky and very much a tease. He'd enjoyed feeling like they'd been best buddies since forever. And then there had been those intimate moments, where they'd traded easy caresses. He could see himself doing that forever with her. She tested him, gave him reason to pause and reflect. And he liked the reflection of himself that he saw in her eyes.

Noah hadn't known his own prowess to this extreme before last night with Catherine. She excited him and kept him excited. Just thinking about her pulled the muscles in his Southern quadrant stiff.

He reached for the bar of soap, lathering his washcloth. As he ran the square of plush fabric over his skin, he tried not to think about Catherine but his best efforts failed. She had his full and undivided attention.

* * *

Naomi passed him a large glass of a green mixture as he moved back into the kitchen.

"I need to order flowers," he said, looking at his sister for assistance.

Naomi eyed him with a raised brow. "For who?"

"You know who. I want roses. Pink ones. Any recommendations for florists?"

"I personally like the Art Floral downtown but the Flower Box is good, too."

He nodded. "Thanks," he said as he walked to the hall closet.

He pulled a locked box from the top shelf and pressed his thumb to the digital pad to unlock it. He pulled his duty weapon from inside, sliding it into the harness under his navy blue blazer.

Moving back to the kitchen, he took another big swig of his breakfast smoothie. His sister was still staring at him, her arms crossed over her chest.

"What now?" he asked, leaning back against the counter.

"You're not even going to give me any details? You spend the weekend with that woman and now you're sending her flowers and I don't get any information? Nothing?"

"I don't kiss and tell, you know that."

"So you did kiss her…"

Noah laughed. "I have to run or I'm going to be late."

"John called," she said, referring to their Texas cousin. "He wanted to know if we're all going to Paris for Natalie and Tinjin's runway show. He said the family is all flying in together if we want to catch a ride."

Noah nodded. His baby sister had left him numerous messages since Friday to ask the same question. "Text me the dates again," he said. "I want to go but I'll need to work out the dates with my new job."

"You decided to take it?" Naomi asked as he headed to the door.

Noah paused, his hand on the doorknob. "Yeah," he said. "I think I have."

Two dozen pink roses sat in a crystal vase atop Catherine's desk. Marvin Lyons, her personal assistant, was spinning them in a circle for the perfect angle. Catherine twisted the accompanying card between her fingers. A wide grin blessed her expression.

"They smell divine!" Marvin chimed. "Who knows pink roses are your favorite?"

She shook her head as she read the card. Her wide grin spread ear to ear.

"Ohh! Who is he?" Marvin questioned, dropping into the seat in front of her desk.

"A very good friend," she answered. "Someone I went to high school with."

"You had a reunion fling! You dirty bird!" Marvin laughed teasingly.

"I did not!"

"Yes, you did. I can see it all over your face."

"What?" Frederick questioned as he entered her

office without knocking. "What are you two talking about?"

"Don't you knock?" Marvin chastised, annoyance spilling from his eyes.

"Shouldn't you be at your desk?" Frederick snapped back.

Catherine and Marvin exchanged a quick look. She took a deep breath, stalling the rising argument.

"I was just telling Marvin about our high school reunion. It was a lot of fun. You should have gone."

Frederick's eyes widened. "I didn't think you were going. You didn't sound like you were interested."

Catherine shrugged. "I changed my mind."

"I wish you had told me. I would have gone with you."

"It was a last-minute decision," Catherine said, meeting his gaze.

He nodded. "I called you this weekend but you didn't call me back. What was that about?" Frederick questioned, sounding like a scorned lover.

A moment of awkward silence passed, and Catherine watched as Marvin looked from her to Frederick, amusement painting his expression.

Catherine could feel her facial muscles tighten as she tried to force a smile back to her face.

"How are we with those financial reports?" she asked, changing the subject.

"The attorneys have everything they need. We'll sit down with them and the accounting team later this week. You should have the numbers to review on your desk by tomorrow morning."

"Good. Marvin, I need the entire executive team here next week. Tell the Atlanta and the Salt Lake City staff that they'll need to be here Tuesday through Thursday. Everyone should make arrangements to fly in Monday night and out on Friday. All the lunches will be in house and they should plan to work. Make reservations for dinner Tuesday only. Wednesday they can all do their own thing."

"Yes, Cat."

"I also want the safety reports for every plane on my desk by tomorrow. And I mean every plane. And I'll need an update from acquisitions. Where are we on the sales of those Cessna Citations? I want two additional Gulfstream G650s ordered by the end of the month and in the registry in the next six weeks."

Marvin jotted notes into his iPad. "The Cessna Citations have sold. Titles transferred to their new owners last week. I'll have an answer on the purchases within the hour. You also have a meeting with the marketing team this afternoon. They want to pitch the print ads."

"Where are they looking to run them? Do we know?" Catherine asked, shifting her gaze back to Frederick.

"I'm not sure," the man answered.

She looked toward Marvin. "I want to know before the meeting and I want a hard copy of each magazine," she said.

Marvin nodded. "I'll take care of it. Anything else, Cat?"

"Check if Laughing Lotus is still doing that lunchtime yoga class. If they are, reserve me a spot, please. Thank you."

With a nod of his head, Marvin paused to sniff the roses one last time. He moved toward the door and made a quick exit.

"Who sent you flowers?" Frederick asked, noticing the arrangement for the first time.

Catherine shrugged.

"You don't know who sent them?" Frederick persisted. A wave of concern suddenly washed over his expression.

"I have a secret admirer," Catherine answered, meeting his stare.

Something in his expression struck a nerve. "What's wrong, Frederick?"

He shook his head. "It's nothing for you to be concerned about. I have it under control."

She stared at him as he tossed her a toothy smile.

Frederick had changed little since high school. He was still awkward, his expensive designer suits masking his small frame. His dark curls lay like a bad shag rug on his head and he had never gotten control of his bad skin. His smile was a perfect exhibit of polished veneers and he had beautiful hazel eyes. But there was something deceptive about his stare. Something off-putting that had always made Catherine question his motives, despite him being one of the best at his job and overwhelmingly loyal.

She gestured to the folders on her desk. "Let's talk later. I have some catching up to do."

Frederick nodded. "Interested in doing an early

dinner? I know someone at Corkbuzz down in Chelsea Market. I hear the fried gnocchi with salami and the spicy clams in chili butter are a must try."

She nodded but didn't bother to respond. She spun around in her chair, facing the credenza behind her. She pulled open a drawer and pretended to search inside. Frederick stood staring for a brief moment before he turned and made his exit.

When the door slammed closed behind him, Catherine spun back around, rising from her seat. She moved to the floral arrangement, inhaling the sweet scent. Noah had sent flowers to her Atlanta office the day before. They'd been waiting for her when she arrived at the Peachtree Road location. His card had been sentimental as he'd thanked her for a weekend that had changed his life.

This bouquet had surprised her, though the card was just as sweet as the first. He'd written that he missed her. Three little words that had made her smile.

She was lost in thoughts of Noah when Marvin burst back into her office. She eyed him curiously as he tossed his hands up in frustration.

"What is it, Marvin?"

"Frederick is going to work my last nerve. The man is a freak. And I hate to tell you again but that fool is stupid in love with you."

Catherine frowned. She'd known Frederick had feelings for her when he'd professed his adoration after a drinking binge one night a few years ago. Her rejection had been swift, using their very successful business alliance to put him off. She considered Frederick a friend and nothing more. She felt no attraction toward the man whatsoever, mostly put off by his arrogant behavior and attitude of entitlement. There wasn't an ice cube's chance in hell of them ever sharing a personal relationship.

She shook her head at Marvin. "Frederick and I have a strictly business relationship. There will never be anything else between us and he knows it. There are some things that just won't work. Office relationships are one of those things."

"Humph!" Marvin chimed. "I hear you talking. But I don't think Frederick is listening. He just ripped me a new one about those flowers like I was the one who sent them to you!"

Commander Derrick Quince sat with his hands folded as Noah announced he was leaving the Salt Lake City police department. His resignation letter sat against Quince's wooden desk. His commanding officer wasn't pleased.

"I don't want to lose you, Stallion. How can we change your mind?"

"It's a done deal, sir. I've enjoyed my tenure here but it's time for me to try something new. This is a great opportunity, and the salary can't be beat. I really don't have any other option."

Quince nodded. "Well, you'll definitely be missed. You're one of the best officers I've ever had the privilege of working with." Moving onto his feet, he extended his hand. "I hate to lose you, Stallion, but I wish you only the very best."

"Thank you, sir," Noah said as the two shook hands.

Minutes later he stood with two of his fellow officers.

"Who's going to lead this team if you're not here, Stallion?"

"Yeah, dude. No one keeps me in line the way you do."

Noah laughed. "You'll be fine. I'm sure they'll have another hard-nosed detective here to watch over you in no time."

Both men shook his hand. The whole department was extending him well wishes when his cell phone vibrated against his hip. He took a quick glance down at the incoming number, then excused himself, retreating into his office.

"Hi."

"Hi. Is this a good time to talk?"

"Anytime you want to talk is a good time."

Catherine smiled on her end of the receiver. "Thank you so much for the beautiful flowers. The roses are absolutely gorgeous. Both arrangements."

"I just wanted to let you know how much I enjoyed our time together. And that I miss you."

"I miss you, too. I'm already trying to figure out when I'll get back to Salt Lake City. Or maybe you can come to New York?"

"That's definitely a possibility."

"I own a plane whenever you're ready."

Noah laughed. "I'll keep that in mind."

There was a moment of pause. "I didn't think this would be so hard," Catherine said, her voice dropping to a low whisper.

Noah nodded, taking a deep inhale. "I know. I hated not being able to talk to you yesterday."

"I apologize for that. After we landed I ran from one meeting to the next. By the time the day ended I was exhausted. Then when I finally reached home, I was out before my head hit the pillow."

"I figured as much, which is why I didn't call you. I didn't want to disturb your rest."

"I really wish you had. I would have loved to have heard your voice," Catherine said.

Noah laughed. "So how's your day been thus far?"

"I can't complain. I'm on the last leg of things to do before the company goes public. It's just a matter of dotting all the i's and crossing my t's."

"It'll work out."

"I know. I'm worrying unnecessarily but it's what I do."

There was a moment of hesitation, and Noah could hear voices in the background. He heard Catherine take a deep breath, inhaling swiftly.

"I have a meeting I need to get to but can I call you later tonight?" she asked. There was nervous anticipation in her tone and it made Noah smile.

"I'd be hurt if you didn't," he responded. "And if you don't call me, I *will* call you."

His home was quiet when he finally arrived back to it that evening. His sister had left him a note on the counter about dinner being in the refrigerator. She had spent a fair amount of time cleaning. The space smelled of pine and lemon. The furniture had been dusted and polished, his carpets vacuumed, his floors swept.

Despite knowing he had a maid service that cleaned twice weekly, Naomi always insisted on cleaning for him when she came into town. He had never once argued against it. His sister's touch always made his house feel more like home.

He sent her a quick text message to say thank-you and to check that she had made it back home safely. After a quick back and forth exchange with her, he slid the plate of meat loaf, mashed potatoes and peas into the microwave to heat. Flipping on the big-screen television, he pulled a stool up to the marble-topped counter and dined.

Domestic violence dominated the news. An occurrence of it had recently hit home when he'd found himself investigating the brutal death of a young woman who'd been previously battered by her husband. Two small children had been left to deal with the aftermath. From start to finish the investigation had wrecked his spirit. He let out a heavy sigh as he moved from his kitchen to the family room sofa.

Leaning back, he lifted his long legs to the ottoman. He closed his eyes, and thoughts of Catherine immediately crossed his mind. He missed her and they had so much to talk about. There had still been no conversations about him going to work for Fly High and it was something they needed to discuss sooner than later. He was accepting their job offer and he didn't know what that would mean for the two of them.

Just as he was pondering the complications, his cell phone chimed, vibrating against the coffee table. Pulling the device into his hands, he smiled. Catherine must have been reading his mind, he thought.

"Hi."

"How are you?" she asked, her voice low and warm like a rich, heavy cream.

"Better now."

"I didn't wake you, did I? I know it's late."

"No, I actually just got in. It's been a long day."

"That doesn't sound good."

"I had a difficult case," he said, his tone indicating it wasn't something he wanted to talk about. "What about your day?" He suddenly looked at his watch. "Why are you up? It's got to be after three in the morning there, right?"

"Yeah, it's late, but taking my company public requires a full twenty-four hour day, seven days per week. It's unending."

"Now explain to me how that works," Noah asked, genuinely interested. "And why are you doing it?"

"Well, I'm doing it because it's my ultimate dream. When I started this business that was one of my end goals and now is the perfect opportunity. It's taken some hard work but I've met the requirements laid out by the investment bank that will underwrite the shares. My growth prospects are high, the service is innovative, we're competitive in the industry and we met the financial audit requirements."

"I was impressed to read that your revenues are as high as they are. You've turned over some serious profits in the last five years."

"The last *nine* years. And I guarantee that we will show a twenty-five percent growth rate over the next five years."

"You really like what you do, don't you?"

"I really do. I was eight years old the first time I flew in a plane. My father and I flew to New York to go to the ballet. Back then I thought I wanted to be a prima ballerina and daddy wanted to show me that I could do anything I put my mind to. The pilot let me into the cockpit and that clinched it for me. Daddy let me get my pilot's license when I turned sixteen, and after I graduated from UCLA he helped me finance my first plane. The business developed from there and from day one I've been committed to making it a success."

"I have no doubts your father is very proud of you."

Noah could feel the magnitude of her smile on the other end of the receiver.

"I can't wait for you both to meet," Catherine said.

"That sounds serious."

She laughed. "It is. I want my two favorite men in the whole wide world to like each other."

"So I'm one of your favorite men?"

"You're high on the list."

He laughed. "Well, I'm sure your father and I will like each other."

"Daddy is going to love you."

Noah smiled. Knowing *of* Catherine's father he wasn't quite sure it would be love but he imagined they could eventually become friendly.

"You should get some rest," he said. "I'm sure you have a long day tomorrow."

"I do but I don't want to stop talking to you. I wish…" She hesitated, suddenly at a loss for words.

There was a wave of silence that swept between them. Noah finally had to prod her on.

"You wish what, baby?"

"I wish I was there with you or you were here with me. I wish I could fall asleep next to you, in your arms."

There was a hint of a whisper in her voice, her tone breathy as if she were fighting not to cry. Noah found himself wishing he could reach through the phone to pull her into his arms. He blew his own deep sigh.

"Are you in bed?" he asked.

"Yes, are you?"

"I'm stretched out on the sofa. This is where I fall asleep most nights."

"That's not good. You should get into your bed. You'll sleep better."

He smiled. "I will, but right now we need to put you to sleep."

"So, how do you propose to do that?"

Noah hesitated only briefly. "Put your phone on speaker and lay it on the pillow beside you," he said.

"Speaker?"

Noah chuckled. "Just do it."

"Okay," Catherine said a moment later.

Noah coughed, then cleared his throat. There was another moment of hesitation and then he began to sing the lyrics to "Hey Jude."

Noah had been told he had an incredible voice. He sang the entire John Lennon and Paul McCartney song, then his own version of Sam Smith's "Nirvana." Both were sweet and melodic, and Noah hoped his voice was doing the trick in lulling her to sleep.

He sang until her breathing had slowed and he could hear her begin to lightly snore. Once he was certain she was asleep, he drifted off with her, leaving the cell phone line between them still open.

Chapter 7

"He sang you to sleep?" Camille asked, incredulous. "Noah sang you to sleep?"

"Why do you say it like that?" Catherine asked. "Hasn't a man ever sung you to sleep?"

Her friend laughed. "My husband's lucky if he can even find a tune, let alone hold one."

"But Doug's a very romantic guy."

"Doug does good which is why I look like a beached whale right now. He has moments when I can't help myself."

Catherine laughed. "You and your husband are having a lot of moments," she said as she called off the names of their children. "Mingus, London, Paris, Basie, Sydney and what are you naming the new babies?"

Camille laughed with her. "I think we're going to name them Brooklyn and Miles. I wanted Bronx for the boy but Doug says I can't name our boy after a place, only a jazz musician. Go figure!"

Catherine continued to howl with laughter as her friend continued. "But we are not talking about me so rewind. We were talking about your stallion singing you to sleep. Sounds to me like your stud has it bad. What's going to happen when you break his heart?"

"I'm not going to break his heart."

"You *always* break their hearts."

Catherine paused as she reflected on her friend's assessment.

"I like Noah. I like him a lot. I want..." She hesitated for a brief second. "I really want to make this relationship work, Camille."

"What have you done with my best friend?" Camille quipped. "The Catherine Moore I know has never before cared about any relationship."

Catherine laughed. "Seriously, Camille, I really like him. The man is male perfection if such a thing exists."

"It doesn't. Ask me how I know."

"How do you know?"

"Because I've been pregnant four times and I have seven kids. There's only been one time that man has knocked me up and only gotten me pregnant with one child. Men are always trying to overcompensate for something so they manage to screw things up. There is no perfect man."

"I told you to cut Doug off after the first set of twins."

"I know but then he does that thing with his tongue and I'm no good."

Both Camille and she laughed heartily.

"When are you coming back to Salt Lake City?"

"I'm not sure yet. Why?"

"When you do, I'll have you and Noah over for dinner. We'll see how he handles my brood. If he's still in one piece after dessert then we'll know he's a keeper."

Catherine giggled. "I already know he's a keeper so I'm not going to subject him to your Chuck E. Cheese's experiment gone wrong."

Catherine spoke to Camille for another few minutes before ending the call, noticing Frederick standing in the middle of her office. As she disconnected the line, she lifted her gaze to his, annoyance furrowing her brow.

"Good morning," he chimed gleefully.

"Frederick."

"Why didn't you call me?" His tone held a hint of attitude.

"Excuse me?"

He took a deep breath. "Sorry. I didn't mean it like that. I had some concerns and when I left you multiple messages and didn't hear back from you I started to worry."

"Why would you be worried, Frederick?"

"Well, with everything that's going on with the

company you're getting some undesirable attention. I was just concerned about your safety."

"What kind of undesirable attention?"

Frederick shook his head. "Nothing that can't be handled and surely nothing for you to be concerned about. That's why you have me."

Catherine stared at him for a brief moment. There was an air of uncertainty that teased her spirit but she wasn't quite sure why. She'd always trusted Frederick, and his business acumen went above and beyond. Deferring to his judgment had never been difficult to do. Until now. She was suddenly guarded, second-guessing herself, as if trusting Frederick so completely hadn't been a good thing after all.

She reached for the intercom on her desk.

"Yes, Catherine?" Marvin's soprano tone chimed through the speakers.

"Marvin, Frederick and I will be taking lunch in the office today. If you'll order me a cobb salad with ranch dressing on the side and a Sprite, please." She looked up at Frederick. "What would you like?"

"I'll take a turkey sub with lettuce, tomato, and extra mayonnaise. A bag of barbecued potato chips and a Coke."

"Did you get that, Marvin?" Catherine questioned, talking back to the speaker.

"I did," Marvin answered.

"Thank you."

She picked up the file folders on her desk, lead-ing the way to the conference room. Frederick followed on her heels.

"We have two planes in Houston that scored low on their inspections," she started. "I want to know why."

"So when are you going to see her again?" Natalie Stallion Braddy questioned.

Noah's little sister had finally caught up with him, their game of phone tag coming to an end.

"Did Naomi call all of you?"

"She called me. But I hear she actually stopped in Los Angeles on her way back to Arizona to tell the twins."

Noah shook his head. "Unbelievable!" he exclaimed. "Is nothing sacred?"

Natalie laughed. "Naomi says you two went to school together but I don't remember who she is."

"You wouldn't," he said. "You were a few years behind us, remember?"

"But I remember the girls the twins use to hang out with."

"Catherine and I never hung out."

"So is she, like..."

Noah interrupted her. "How's Tinjin?"

"My husband has been a busy, busy man. You guys are all coming for the runway show, right?"

"I'm going to try but I can't promise you anything. I start my new job next week."

"You're going to hate it."

"Why would you say that?"

"You're not built for a desk job. It's going to drive you crazy."

"I'll be fine, Natalie."

"Don't say I didn't warn you."

Noah's head shook as his sister caught him up on her latest antics. She was happy and he could hear the joy in her voice. It made him smile.

"So are you going to tell me anything about this woman? Because Naomi says she has your nose wide open. So you should tell me a little something."

Her brother laughed. "You and Naomi are real nuisances."

"That's what sisters are for. So spill the tea."

He took a deep breath. "Catherine is a very successful entrepreneur running a multi-million-dollar company. She's beautiful, intelligent, kindhearted, and funny. She's the whole package."

"Did you really spend the weekend with her?"

"We spent some time together catching up while she was in town."

"Is that what you men are calling it these days?"

"Calling what?"

"You know what…"

"I'm not having this conversation with you, Natalie."

"Why not?"

"Because it's not the kind of conversation a man has with his baby sister."

"You use to change my diapers. We should be able to talk about everything."

"You should be able to talk to me about everything. *My* everything isn't any of your concern."

"Oh, I see how you are!" Natalie laughed. "Well, let me ask the Noah Stallion handbook of questions. Is she good to you?"

Noah chuckled, nodding as if his sister could see him. "She is."

"Is she good for you?"

"Most definitely."

"Will she make you chicken noodle soup when you have a cold?"

"I think she will."

"And if there's a booger in her nose or spinach in her teeth will you wipe it off for her without making a face?"

"I don't know about all that now."

"You are such a man."

"Boogers? Really?"

"It doesn't matter. If she's the one, you should be willing to do whatever it takes."

Noah could only imagine the expression on his face. He could only have this conversation with his favorite baby sister.

"I think she's very special and I like what's developing between us."

"So it's not just a sex thing?"

"No, it's not."

"Because a sex thing wouldn't be bad. Tinjin was a sex thing until he started acting right."

"Too much information, Natalie. I did not need to know that about you and your husband."

Noah could tell by his sister's laugh that she was finding much amusement in making him squirm.

"Seriously," Natalie said, her tone shifting, "I just want to make sure she makes you happy."

"She really does."

"Then I can't wait to meet her. Maybe you can bring her to Paris? You would definitely get the goodies in Paris!"

"Good night, Natalie. I love you!"

"I love you, too, Noah. I'll call you next week to see how the new job is going."

Chapter 8

Frederick met Noah in the lobby of Fly High's Salt Lake City office. The man was flustered as he extended his hand in greeting.

"Noah, welcome to Fly High. I look forward to working with you."

"I appreciate that. I'm excited to get started."

"Let me show you to your new office," Frederick said, gesturing for Noah to follow behind him.

He tossed Noah a look over his shoulder. His eyes were bloodshot and swollen as if he'd been crying. Dark circles outlined the lower lids. Noah guessed the man was simply exhausted.

"Your timing couldn't be better," Frederick said, his tone short. "We have a situation."

"What kind of situation?" Noah asked.

Frederick hesitated, the gesture almost exaggerated. "It might be nothing," he said finally. "But I would prefer to be safe than sorry."

He pointed Noah into a spacious office with a bay of windows that looked out over the city.

"This is your office. In house here you have a team of seven security members who report directly to you and you'll meet them all right after you're done with personnel. There are also safety team coordinators based at each of our private hangers to ensure plane security and then of course there's a whole other staff who are responsible for our digital security. They will report to you, as well."

Noah nodded. "You still haven't told me what the problem is."

Frederick took a deep breath. "I'm worried that someone might be trying to hurt Catherine."

Noah's entire afternoon was spent studying the ins and outs of Fly High's security programs. It took less than an hour to learn who was who on his team and what they did. The rest of his time was spent deciphering Frederick's cryptic concerns.

Noah spun around in his leather executive's chair to stare out the window. One solitary electronic message had been the cause of Frederick's alarm, one line of email message that had been intercepted off their messaging server. What had alarmed Noah most wasn't the message itself but Frederick's handling of things.

"Do you always take it upon yourself to intercept and read other employee's private messages?" he'd asked.

Frederick had bristled. "It's my responsibility to ensure nothing interferes with the operation of this company. Catherine has worked too hard for anything or anyone to disparage the organization or cast any doubts on our integrity. It's paramount that management keeps a finger on what's going on and if that means reading private messages then so be it. We're about to go public so it's even more important now."

Noah's gaze had narrowed but he hadn't responded. There was no way anyone could convince him that the man's irrational paranoia was a tangible reason to intrude on any employee's privacy, most especially the CEO of the company. One of his first acts in his new position would be to shut unnecessary personnel out of the computer servers, and he suspected Frederick wasn't going to take the change lightly.

Noah turned back to his desk and the documents that rested on top. Apparently, the message in question had been one of many, the first coming months earlier, and Catherine had yet to be told. He read the text one more time, the words *I'm coming for you* embedded in his mind. The email message had been sent from an unknown IP address to Catherine's private email account.

He wasn't sure what to make of any of it but he knew that Frederick's idea of handling the situation and his were worlds apart. If Catherine were legitimately in danger, keeping her in the dark wouldn't serve her well. If he needed to keep her safe, she needed to know exactly what he knew. Frederick wasn't going to take kindly to that either, but Noah didn't care. Frederick wasn't his concern. Catherine was.

One week later Noah's trip to New York City had been his first flight on a private aircraft. Not having to use the commercial travel terminal at the airport and having the whole plane to himself had been a new experience. He now understood firsthand what was so unique about the Fly High brand.

The professionalism of the entire crew had been beyond expectation. From the ground crew to the flight staff, everyone had gone above and beyond. When he had landed, a limo had been there to take him to Fly High's Manhattan office.

Hours later, despite his best efforts, Noah had trouble remembering the names of half the staff members he'd met. As the executive team sat in the oversized conference room awaiting Catherine's arrival he was duly impressed with the group she had handpicked to help run her company. It took little time to recognize most were loyal to a fault and they all wanted to see Catherine and the company succeed.

She was laughing when she came into the room. The lilt of it caused Noah to inhale swiftly. Holding his breath, he struggled to stall the quiver of emotion that had suddenly curdled his insides, fighting to not let his feelings show on his face.

Catherine came to an abrupt stop when she saw him. Her bright smile froze on her face, a brief moment of confusion washing over her expression. Her gaze shifted quickly between Noah and Frederick then back to Noah. Her hesitation was swift enough to not be noticed, but Noah didn't miss how her brow had furrowed as she had met his gaze.

He let out the breath he'd been holding, suddenly wondering what he'd gotten himself into. Leaning back in his seat he folded his hands in his lap and eyed her back.

"Well, good morning," Catherine said in greeting, her smile less tense as she took a seat at the head of the table.

Everyone seated around her chimed back in unison. "Good morning."

"Let's get right to business," she started, gesturing in his direction. "First, I want to welcome Noah Stallion to the company. Noah is our new vice president of security operations and he'll be overseeing all aspects of our company security. He'll divide his time between our three corporate locations as well as our satellite hangars. Please give him your full support as he transitions in." She met his gaze, her smile widening. She nodded in his direction, just the slightest tilt of her head.

A round of congratulations circled the table as everyone welcomed him aboard.

Catherine continued. "I want to thank each of you for all the extra effort you've put forth these past few months. I'm very proud of what we've been able to accomplish together. Effective on Monday our company stock will be offered to the public and all of you around this table will be very wealthy."

Another round of applause rang through the room. Noah felt an air of pride wash over him as he watched her. She was authoritative and masterful. She commanded the room and it wasn't hard to see that her staff held her in high esteem. They had a lot of respect for her. The meeting lasted for about an hour before Catherine excused them all.

She gestured toward Noah. "Mr. Stallion, if you'll meet me in my office in thirty minutes, please. I'd like to brief you on a few concerns I have."

Noah nodded. "Not a problem, Ms. Moore."

As he closed the conference room door behind him he heard her slam her pen and pad to the table, her tone seething as she lit into Frederick, who had lagged behind. With the door closed you could only hear her raised voice but it wasn't clear what was being said. Noah stood there listening for only a brief moment before turning and heading back to his office.

Thirty minutes later, Catherine's assistant waved him inside the executive space. As he entered, Catherine rose from her seat and secured the office door. Before he could comment she was in his arms, her mouth locked firmly to his. The kiss was deep and passionate, his excitement abundant. When she finally pulled herself from him they were both breathless. She rested her head against his chest, her arms wrapped tightly around his waist.

"Why didn't you tell me you took the job?"

"I've been trying to tell you since I signed your offer letter, but you didn't want to talk about business, remember? You changed the subject every time I brought it up. Besides, I figured you and Frederick would have discussed it."

Catherine sighed, still hugging him tightly. She didn't want to admit that she'd ignored Frederick, too, but she had, not wanting to think about what would happen with the two of them once Noah became an employee.

Noah continued. "Does it matter? You were the one who said we could be adults about it."

She took a deep breath. "We can but you really need to forewarn a girl. It took everything I had not to throw myself at you in front of everyone. It took me a minute to get my thoughts together."

Noah chuckled softly. "Is that why you just tore Frederick a new one?"

She shook her head. "No. He screwed something else up. I don't know what's going on with him lately but he's making some major mistakes."

Catherine didn't miss the look that crossed Noah's face. "What's wrong? You look concerned."

He shook his head as he pointed her toward her desk. As she took her seat, he unlatched the office door and moved to the chair opposite her desk. "We have some things we need to discuss. I've implemented some new security features that you need to know about."

When Marvin knocked on her office door an hour

later, peeking his head through the entrance, Catherine was still trying to wrap her mind around the fact that her second in command had purposely read and kept private email messages from her. The information was disconcerting, and she found herself questioning what else he might have been holding back. Her head moved slowly from side to side as she tried to make sense out of nonsense. She lifted her hand toward her assistant, her index finger telling him to hold his thoughts a moment longer.

"And the server is now locked?" she asked, her gaze focused on Noah's face.

Noah nodded. "Only two people can access any messages across the company's network. You, and your vice president of information technology. And he understands that if he compromises your trust he's out the door."

"Do you think I need to be worried about those messages?"

Noah shook his head. "No. I'm not going to let anything happen to you."

She nodded. "I want you to stay here in New York until after the stock market launch next week."

He nodded. "I can do that."

She nodded with him, lifting her gaze toward the door. "Yes, Marvin?"

"You're going to be late for your yoga class, Cat."

"Yoga?" Noah mouthed the word, his back to the man at the door. His eyes wide as he looked at her.

She rolled her eyes, trying to keep her expression blank. "Thank you, Marvin. I'm almost done here," she said.

Marvin looked from her to Noah, who still had not turned in his direction. As Catherine waved him out he did an about-face and closed the door behind him.

"Where are you staying?" Catherine asked.

"I'm told I have a room at the Marriott."

She nodded as she reached into the bottom drawer of her desk for her purse. "Check in and then grab a taxi to my place. Here's the key," she said as she jotted her address down on a piece of paper. "I'll meet you there after my class."

"Ms. Moore," Noah said, his voice dropping to a seductive lull. "Whatever do you have planned?"

She smiled. "It's strictly business, Mr. Stallion. Strictly business."

Chapter 9

Catherine's Gramercy Park address was a sleek, custom-designed residence offering over eight thousand square feet of living space, four exposures, sixty-four windows and eighty feet of park frontage. The views were breathtaking, stretching over shaded park lawns, sumptuous foliage, historic neighborhood architecture and up Lexington Avenue, highlighted by the iconic Chrysler Building.

There was a dramatic gallery area showcasing an impressive collection of cobalt-blue glass. Also an expansive, highly polished wood bar and fully stocked wine room, a substantial private library and a home theater, eight bedrooms with marble-tiled baths, a gourmet kitchen and finishing touches that included hand-troweled walls and ceilings, rift and quartered white oak flooring, a twenty-four-hour doorman, full-time concierge, a sleek spa and fitness center and two rooftop terraces. The decor was polished and elegant with hints of warmth and ambiance that had Catherine written all over it. Noah found himself both impressed and overwhelmed by it all.

He stood staring out the window when Catherine entered the apartment. He turned in her direction as she made her way through the front door.

"Honey, I'm home!" she chimed, a hint of humor in her tone.

Noah laughed softly as he opened his arms wide, and Catherine stepped easily into them. He kissed her lips, not knowing how much he'd missed their touch until they were once again pressed tight to his.

"How was your yoga class?" he asked when they finally parted.

Catherine moved to drop her purse to the coffee table. "I couldn't focus. All I could think about was getting back here to you."

Noah nodded. He gestured around the space as he took a seat beside her on the sofa. "This is some place, Ms. Moore. I love the views."

She smiled. "That's probably the only thing about the place that I truly like. I like my Atlanta home much more."

"How many homes do you have?"

"I have property in five states and two properties overseas. But they're houses. The Atlanta property is the only one I'd really consider a home."

Noah draped an arm around her waist. "Tell me about it. What makes it so special?"

Catherine paused, and Noah didn't miss the tears that suddenly misted her eyes. He trailed his hand along the side of her face, concern painting his expression. It was a brief moment before she finally responded.

"It was my nana's house. She passed away a few years ago and she left the property to me. It's not big at all, just over a thousand square feet. But it sits on ten acres of land and has a huge front porch. It's really just a very special place. I have a lot of great memories there."

"Maybe I'll get to see it someday."

Catherine cut a quick eye at him then shifted her gaze to the floor. "You say that like you have some doubts."

He shrugged. "No. Not really. I just know that we have a very unique situation."

"It's not that unique."

"It is to me."

There was something in Noah's voice that moved her to lift her eyes back to his. There was a look of dismay on his face and his brow furrowed. Her gaze was questioning as she met his stare.

"I don't lie," he said. "And it's not in my nature to keep secrets. And I definitely don't make a point of hiding my feelings about a woman I care about. So this is, well…out of my comfort zone. And I don't like it, Cat. I don't like it one bit."

Catherine nodded her head slowly. She opened

her mouth to speak but then closed it, not sure if she should say anything at all. The quiet in the room was thick and she suddenly felt awkward.

She really hadn't thought about the ramifications of hiding what was going on between them. She just knew that a relationship with someone on her staff went against everything she had always preached and practiced. Even with all that had happened between them since the reunion she truly hadn't considered the magnitude of dating a man who worked for her. All she'd been thinking about was how much she loved the time they shared, wanting nothing more than to be with Noah.

Catherine shifted her body closer to his, moving to lean her head against his chest. "I'm sorry," she said softly. "But I don't know what else to do. This has caught me completely off guard. I just didn't expect to feel the way that I do about you."

"And how's that? How do you feel about me, Cat?"

She took a deep breath. "Like I'm the luckiest woman in the world."

Wrapping his arms around her, he hugged her close. "We'll figure it out," he said, certainty fueling his words. "Somehow we'll make it work for us."

She smiled. "I could always fire you."

Noah chuckled softly. "You could definitely do that."

"But you're good. If it weren't for you I wouldn't have known about Frederick and my mail."

"I am good so firing me really isn't an option right

now. You need me until after your stock launch. Then you're going to need me after that, too."

She nodded. "I probably will."

"You definitely will. I'm not going to go any place just yet."

She smiled as she tilted her head up to kiss his lips. "I'm glad we got that settled."

He shrugged, the slightest smile on his face. But something about his expression told Catherine that nothing had really been settled at all.

"So are you going to at least feed me?" Noah questioned. "I'm hungry."

Catherine laughed. "I can definitely feed you but I think you actually have a meal budget. We can go out and you can treat."

Noah laughed with her. "I do have a food budget but I'm saving it."

She eyed him curiously. "For what?"

"Dessert."

Confusion washed over Catherine's expression. "Dessert?"

He nodded as he leaned forward to kiss her lips. "For those days the boss can't give me any of her sugar. My budget will come in handy then."

Catherine cooked the evening meal, and Noah admitted to being surprised by her skills in the kitchen. After close to thirty minutes of slinging pots and pans across the marble counters, she served him a meal of stewed chicken with baby carrots and red potatoes. The food was good, paired with crusty bread and a bottle of Pinot Grigio.

Their conversation was light and easy as they bantered back and forth, the teasing a refreshing diversion from the seriousness of their earlier conversation. Catherine had a mischievous side that Noah found engaging and her lighthearted playfulness awakened a side of himself that he had never fully explored. When she'd cajoled him into doing a series of musical impressions, singing a Michael Jackson song then a Barry White tune, they'd both laughed until their sides had ached.

Noah pointed his index finger at her. "Okay, it's your turn."

She held up her hands as if she were surrendering. "Oh, no. I don't sing. I don't even pretend to sing when I'm in the shower."

"Everyone sings. Give me some Alicia Keys."

"I can't do Alicia Keys."

"Then go old-school. Sing some Diana Ross or Whitney Houston."

Catherine laughed. "I am not singing!"

Noah eased to her side and began to tickle her stomach. "Sing for me. You'll sing for me, right?"

She laughed, pushing his hands away as they danced across her abdomen. "Stop, Noah! I am not singing."

He leaned back against his seat, crossing his arms over his chest. He feigned a look of disappointment, his full lips pouting profusely.

"Don't give me that look," Catherine said, still giggling.

He pushed his bottom lip out even farther as he held up his index finger. "One song?" he said.

Catherine rolled her eyes. Her whole body shivered with glee, her laughter rich and warm. It was the sweetest music to Noah's ears.

"Okay," she said, finally acquiescing. "One song."

Noah grinned, shifting upright as he twisted his body toward her.

Catherine began to bob her head up and down, grabbing a silent beat in her head. Noah's grin widened even more.

As Catherine began to sing the old Meghan Trainor summer anthem, Noah laughed out loud. She was off-key but spirited as she jumped to her feet to emphasize her routine with a side-to-side shimmy. His head bobbed up and down against his broad shoulders as he snapped his fingers along with her.

By the conclusion of her performance, complete with much hip action and booty shaking, the two were laughing hysterically. The sound of their cheerful voices bounced from room to room as the duo sang, danced and chased each other from room to room. By the end of the night when both had slipped between the sheets of Catherine's king-size bed, exhaustion had claimed them both.

Catherine sighed deeply as she rolled her body against his, laying her head on his chest. She was warm and comfortable against him, the rise and fall of his breathing like the sweetest lullaby. As Noah tightened his arms around her torso, she snuggled even closer against him and before either could count to ten they were both lost in a deep, dream-filled slumber.

Catherine and Noah were still laughing as they stepped out of a yellow cab in front of the Fly High corporate offices the next morning.

Stepping out of his own taxi, Frederick eyed them both curiously. "Good morning," he said, his eyes shifting from one to the other. "Did I miss a breakfast meeting or something?" he questioned.

Noah pressed a warm palm against Catherine's lower back as he returned the new day greeting. "Good morning."

Catherine met the man's stare, her smile cresting downward. "No, Frederick, you didn't," she said, a hint of attitude in her tone. Her body tensed and annoyance creased her forehead.

Frederick nodded, still eyeing them both curiously.

"Deep breaths," Noah muttered, his words a low whisper. His eyes flicked back and forth, taking in everything around them.

Frederick didn't miss the gesture, bristling as he watched Catherine lean back against Noah's touch. He looked from her to him and back, his gaze narrowing until his eyes were thin slits.

"Why don't we go inside," Noah said, gently nudging Catherine forward. "I need to speak to you both about the changes I've made to some of our security protocols."

Frederick bristled even more. "Changes? You don't have the authority to make changes without running them by me first."

"Noah reports directly to me," Catherine said tersely. "He has whatever authority I give him and I've given him the authority to do whatever he feels necessary to safeguard this company."

"I know, Cat, but…" Frederick stammered.

She glanced down to her wristwatch, cutting off his comment. "I have a few items I need to take care of and then we can talk," she said, meeting Frederick's gaze evenly. She extended the hint of a smile. "I'll see you in my office in about thirty minutes."

With a quick nod of his head, Frederick rushed ahead of them.

Noah shook his head. "You've scared him."

"He should be scared. At the moment I'm seriously considering firing him. I want to hear what our legal department has to say first." She sighed.

The two entered the building together. Noah suddenly felt as if everyone was staring at them, seeming to know their secret and then he realized he still had an arm around her waist. He snatched the appendage away, grabbing at his attaché with both hands. Catherine laughed as he took an abrupt step away from her.

"That didn't look too obvious." Catherine giggled softly.

Noah rolled his eyes. "I don't know how to do this," he responded.

She took a deep breath and nodded. "Just do what feels right, Noah. I don't think either one of us can go wrong if we just do what we know is right."

Smiling, Noah nodded his head. They'd come to the entrance of her office, and Marvin greeted them both, standing with Catherine's requisite cup of Starbucks coffee in hand. Noah leaned to kiss her cheek, then turning, he gave Marvin a quick wave of his hand.

"Thirty minutes," Catherine called after him.

He turned, his grin miles wide. "Yes, ma'am!"

Their conversation with Frederick was tense and heated. Neither Catherine nor Noah had expected the hostility and rage that had come from the man.

"This company is where it is because of me!" Frederick had shouted.

Catherine had bristled in response, her index finger waving in his direction. "You manipulating what I see and don't see didn't build this business. Get that straight. The success of Fly High was manifested long before I ever considered bringing you aboard, and you damn well better remember that!"

"So what now?" Frederick snapped. He glared in Noah's direction. "You hire your pretty boyfriend and suddenly everything I've done for you doesn't mean anything?"

Noah shifted forward in his seat, his gaze narrowed as he met the look the other man was giving him.

Catherine held up her palm to stall the comment on the tip of his tongue. "That depends on you, Frederick," she said. "From this point forward you will only do as I direct or I'll gladly accept your resignation today. Now, we have always worked well together and I want to trust that we can continue to but that depends on you."

Frederick's tone suddenly changed, emotion sweeping over his composure. "You know I would never do anything to hurt you, Catherine. I was only trying to help. I was only trying to do what was best for you and the business."

Catherine took a deep breath. "I know. That's the only reason you still have a job."

Frederick pulled his shoulders back as he buttoned his suit jacket, adjusting it around his thin frame. "I need to prep for our final meeting with the underwriters. Do you have any other concerns that need to be addressed?"

Catherine stared. "Just one. If you ever deign to make a snide comment about Noah, me or our relationship again, it will be the last time you do so as an employee of Fly High. Is that understood?"

Frederick shot Noah another harsh look before turning his gaze back toward her. With only a quick nod of his head he turned and exited the room.

Noah shot Catherine a look. "Well, that went well."

She shrugged as she moved back behind her desk

to her computer. "I'd say it went better than I initially expected. His feelings are hurt but he'll get over it."

"Let's hope so."

A dark cloud suddenly crossed Catherine's face. She began to visibly shake and concern washed over Noah's spirit.

"What is it? What's wrong?"

She turned her computer screen in his direction. A lengthy list of email messages lined the screen, each having the same subject, the words I'M COMING FOR YOU in big bold letters.

Noah walked the halls of Fly High with the security guard, an elderly man everyone called Bishop. The old geezer was a wealth of information about the inner workings of the company and its employees. The two had made the rounds, checking that doors were secure and no one was where they had no business being. They also engaged in conversation, Bishop having something to say about everything.

Bishop wished him a good night as they found themselves back at the door of Catherine's office. He poked his head inside the door and waved. "You take care of yourself now, Miss Cat. I'll be back around in another hour and I'll check if you're still here."

Catherine waved. "Thanks, Bishop. Tell your wife I said hello."

The old man nodded his gray head. "I'll do that. Been trying to get her to make you some of her banana pudding that you like but she been having problems with her blood pressure and ain't been feeling so good."

"Well, don't you bother her about making me banana pudding. Your wife likes me and I won't have you messing things up!" she teased.

The old man laughed. He pointed in Noah's direction. "Make sure the boss lady gets home safe, please."

Noah nodded. "Yes, sir. I will do that."

The two men shook hands. Noah then stood in the doorway, watching as he moved back down the hall and out of sight.

"Anyone else still here?" Catherine asked. She stole a quick glance at her watch, noting that it was well after ten o'clock in the evening.

He shook his head. "Just you, me, and Mr. Bishop. Frederick even hightailed it out of here early."

"He's still hot with me."

"I don't think so. I think he felt vindicated when I told him about the emails."

"You told him?"

Noah nodded. "I had some questions about the earlier ones."

Catherine sighed. "I'm scared, Noah. And I really don't scare easy. Why would someone be doing this to me?"

He took a deep breath as he shook his head. "I don't know. But I'm going to find out."

She nodded but didn't bother to respond, her mind seeming to drift off into thought. Noah watched her, awed by her composure. Catherine's air of authority was complemented by her generous spirit. She was enthralling and possessed a unique sense of self that few others possessed. She suddenly shifted her eyes in his direction and smiled.

"What?" she questioned, the lines of her profile softening.

He shook his head. "I was just thinking how beautiful you are."

Her smile widened, her lips parting ever so slightly as she stared back. "Are you off duty yet, Mr. Stallion?"

"I don't know. I'll have to ask my boss."

She nodded as she rose from her seat and moved to where he stood. She gripped the front of his suit jacket with both hands as she moved against him, tilting her face upward. "You will officially be off the clock the minute you kiss me."

With one hand, he brushed the length of her hair from her face. His eyes danced with hers, the two studying each other intently. He leaned forward, and then hesitated before leaning forward once again, allowing his lips to dance over her cheek.

"A kiss like that?" he whispered.

Catherine chuckled. "Did you mean it? You have to kiss me like you really mean it."

He nodded, amusement dancing in his stare. This time he wrapped his arms around her and pulled her close. He held her tight, saying nothing as he nestled her body against his own. He dropped his face to hers, a slow descent until he met her lips, kissing her intently. Their mouths danced in perfect sync, the beat of their hearts drumming a rich, warm beat in the background. When they finally parted, both were panting heavily.

"How was that?" Noah muttered as he trailed his tongue across the line of her lips, then kissed the tip of her nose.

She nodded. "Oh, yeah. That's what I'm talking about."

Noah laughed heartily. He shook his head as Catherine giggled with him. His gaze skated to the view outside, the building across the way illuminated so that they could see inside. Someone sat in an empty office, focused in a stack of papers that decorated a desktop.

"Do you have blinds that you can close?" he asked, gesturing toward the glass.

Catherine shook her head. "No, but the glass is covered with a privacy film. You can only see inside if the lights are on the highest setting. With just that desk lamp on you can't see anything. Why?"

Noah shrugged his shoulders slightly as he shifted his eyebrows skyward.

Catherine's smile pulled wide and full across her face as she read the thoughts that crossed his mind. She bit down against her lower lip as Noah moved back to the door and locked it. She watched as he moved to the windows to stare across the way and then down to the ground below. He turned toward her and gestured with his index finger.

His come-hither stare made Catherine gasp slightly as she moved to his side. She took a breath and held it as he pushed the folders on her desk to the side. He turned, dropping both his hands against the expanse of her hips, his hands gently gliding over her lush curves. Before she realized it he'd undone the zipper to her skirt, the garment quickly falling to the floor beneath her feet. She was now standing in nothing but a cobalt-blue thong and matching bra beneath her black satin blouse. In one swift motion Noah lifted her to the desktop. The wooden surface felt chilly against the cheeks of her buttocks.

Standing over her, Noah slowly undid the pearl-shaped buttons on her blouse, pushing the smooth fabric off her shoulders. She smiled as he unsnapped her bra, pushing it up to expose her breasts. The lush tissue stood at full attention and as he leaned forward her nipple grazed against his lips. She whimpered softly, his touch like an easy breeze. He circled the chocolate button with his tongue, gently sucking and licking one and then the other. He lavished damp, heated kisses against her skin as she cupped his face in her palms and guided him from one to the other.

Catherine whimpered again, the lustful sound heated with passion. Her hands dropped against his shoulders, nudging him downward. He kissed a slow path down her belly, and her breathing quickened. Noah suddenly dropped his body down into her leather executive's chair, pulling himself up between her legs as he palmed her kneecaps, his touch teasing. He looked up and met her gaze, his eyes announced his intentions.

Catherine gasped again, a rush of air blowing past her lips as his hands eased past her parted knees, his fingers trailing heavily along her inner thighs. When his fingertips reached her sweet spot, easing past the line of her lace G-string, she purred loudly.

"You are so wet," Noah exclaimed, the scent of her arousal teasing his nostrils. "It feels so good."

She clutched her arms over her chest, her hands rubbing her breasts. "You make me wet," she muttered as she played with her own nipples. She flicked them with her fingertips.

Noah smiled up at her as he continued his ministrations.

"Taste me," Catherine said suddenly, her eyes wide, her voice low and husky.

Her feminine spirit glistened with moisture beneath her neatly trimmed bush. Noah dipped his hand back in and raised two fingers to his lips, wrapping his tongue around them as he sucked them into his mouth. Her taste mixed with the lingering remnants of the spearmint gum he'd had earlier.

Catherine heard herself gasp as she watched him. He began to kiss a damp path up her thigh, the decadent scent luring him in. "That's it," she murmured softly, her hands reaching out to stroke his face as he drew closer to his goal. His touch was heated and her body quivered in anticipation. She lifted her hips as he pulled at her silk undergarment and a wicked chill shot down the length of her spine.

She purred, over and over, a growing need fueling the lust that heated her skin and the blood coursing through her veins. Her moans were more persistent, and Noah could no longer resist. His lips pressed to her sex, his tongue instinctively slipping inside the soft folds, slowly lapping at her. His hands stroked the undersides of Catherine's thighs as his tongue began to tease and taunt her feminine spirit. He was eager to please her, lost in a state of hypnotic arousal. He reveled in the taste and feel of her, his tongue alternating between her wet lips and the rapidly swelling bud of her clit.

Moans of her pleasure encouraged him on as her hands gripped the back of his head. Her eyes were closed, rolled back in her head. She lifted her hips from the desktop, pushing herself against his mouth. Noah lapped at her hungrily as if his life was sustained solely by the nectar flowing from her secret place, her passion and need the key that opened her to him.

The pleasure was unending as currents of electricity shot through her. And then she was there, her back arching as she pulled him in deep with her hands on the back of his head, his hands held her firm bottom as her juices surged. Noah drank as if his life depended on it, moaning as intensely as she did. Her body quivered and shook and then she cried out, every muscle jerking as her climax rushed through, rewarding him with more of her delicious taste and scent.

He was reluctant as he was pushed away from her sex, wanting to stay there until he could do no more. But Catherine's grip was firm and strong, shifting him back against the cushioned seat as she clasped her knees tightly together, riding the last fringes of her orgasm.

Catherine smiled at him, her eyes looking over Noah's body as though she was a predator assessing her next meal. She shivered as the heat between her legs intensified with a vengeance, her body craving more. Sliding off the desk, she fumbled with his belt buckle, and then his zipper, pushing his slacks down until she freed him from his pants. His erection was full and abundant as she bounced the fullness of him against her palm.

Noah reached into the inner pocked of his blazer, drawing his wallet into his hand. He pulled a pro-phylactic from an inside compartment and passed it to her. Without a word, she sheathed him quickly then eased her body into his lap and dropped her-self against him.

The ride was swift, quick and dirty. She rode him hard, slamming her body against his as her inner walls stroked him tightly. She rode him like it would be her last ride, as if his leaving her body would frac-ture her heart and leave her broken. She rode him fast, then slow, and then fast again. She rode him gently, then she rode him with every fiber of her being, her body bucking against him voraciously. He screamed her name, muffling the sound into her chest as she clutched his head between her breasts. She rode him until they were both spent, believing she could never again move another muscle.

It wasn't quite midnight when Noah and Cath-erine found their way to the building's lobby. Bishop sat at the front desk, his eyes glued on the panel of security screens. The muffled sounds from an old transistor present in the background.

Catherine laughed, tilting her head toward Noah. "We all chipped in and bought Bishop an iPod last year but he loves that old radio."

Bishop nodded. "Yep! I sure do. It works good and I ain't got to figure out all the buttons."

Noah laughed, giving the old man two thumbs-up.

Catherine shook her head. "One day, Bishop, we're going to bring you into this century. You'll be amazed at the new technology."

"Little lady, I'm good right where I am. Life is simple and a man couldn't ask for anything more. You young people like to complicate things and then you're unhappy when it don't work or it don't work the way you want it to. I can't get with all that drama. Keep it simple!"

"You might be on to something," she said, leaning to kiss his cheek.

He gave her a wink of his eye, a blush of color heating his dark cheeks.

Catherine smiled as she slipped her hand into Noah's. "Well, you have a good night, Bishop."

The old man gave them both a toothy grin. "You, too, Miss Moore. Young man, you keep her safe, you hear me?" He pointed a wrinkled finger at Noah.

Noah nodded. "Hold down the fort, Mr. Bishop. I'm counting on you."

"Yes, sir! I got this!"

Chapter 10

After a late-night meal, Noah and Catherine found themselves showered and changed and lost in piles of paperwork. Catherine had spread a host of documents across the dining-room table, and Noah was situated on the sofa reviewing a stack of reports that had crossed his desk. He had never fathomed the volume of paperwork the position entailed but he was grateful that most of it was at least interesting.

In the distance the soft lull of a neighbor playing blues echoed around the room. The music was mournful and for the brief moment he'd bothered to focus on the lyrics, it almost saddened him. Noah let out a soft sigh as he flipped through one folder, something out of sync catching his eye. He swung his legs off the couch and sat upright. "Cat, how often do you have the flight logs audited?"

She looked up from her own paperwork. "Annually. Why?"

He shook his head. "Just curious," he muttered, his eyes shifting between two documents.

She leaned back in her seat, pulling a pair of black-rimmed reading glasses from her face. She dropped her hands into her lap. "Frederick doesn't think it's necessary but I use a third-party company to do the field audits. Typically, he'll review the reports and gives me an overview."

"Have you ever had any problems?"

She shook her head. "There was only one time something was red-flagged. But that was a few years ago. The pilot's logs didn't match. Apparently, he was fudging his flight hours and taking the plane places we weren't aware of. The system was done manually back then and too much was being recorded by hand. That's what triggered me to computerize all of our systems. I knew I needed a better system of checks and balances in place. Hasn't been a problem since."

Noah nodded. A blanket of silence filled the space between them as he pondered what he needed and how he would achieve his plan. "I want to fly down to the Texas hub tomorrow," he said finally, still staring at the documents in his hand.

"Did you find something? What's wrong?" Catherine questioned. She rose from her seat, moving in his direction.

"It may be nothing but I want to check it out. I

don't want to raise any alarms just yet, especially if it turns out that I'm wrong." He lifted his gaze to hers.

Catherine stood staring at him, reflecting on his words. She trusted him, so she didn't need to ask him anything else. She nodded. "I'll send Marvin a text and have him arrange a flight first thing in the morning. Will you need to stay overnight?"

Noah shook his head. "No. I should be able to come back tomorrow night."

"Good." She smiled, extending her hand toward him. "Because I would miss you. Are you ready to go to bed?"

Smiling back he entwined his fingers between hers. "I'm ready when you are."

"Good, because I'm exhausted and you need to sing me to sleep again."

Noah chuckled softly. "I can do that."

As they turned off the lights and headed toward the bedroom, one last thought crossed Noah's mind.

"Yes?" Catherine asked as he called her name.

"Don't tell Frederick where I'm going or why."

Catherine stared at him for a moment before she nodded her assent.

"Where's Stallion?" Frederick snapped as he stomped into the conference room.

Catherine lifted her eyes from the spreadsheets that lay across the conference room table. "Good morning to you, too," she responded.

Frederick took a deep breath. "Sorry. Good morning."

"Now, what's the problem?" she said, gracing him with a half smile.

"I wanted to talk to Noah. To see where we are with those email threats you received. I stopped by the Marriott hotel, but they said he checked out two days ago. His secretary said he didn't come in this morning but she doesn't know where he is. So I thought you might know."

She nodded as she gestured for him to take a seat. "He's doing something for me to prepare for Monday. He'll be back in the office tomorrow."

Catherine could see Frederick's mind racing. He wanted to ask what Noah was doing for her but he didn't. Instead, he shifted his eyes to her face, tossing her a hint of a smile.

"I was just reviewing these final numbers," she said. "Everything appears to be in order. We should do very well next week."

Frederick nodded. "I'm glad I can share this experience with you, Cat. You know how much you mean to me."

"I do, which is why I want to apologize to you for overreacting the other day. I know that you were only trying to protect the company and me. But I can't have you doing things behind my back. I can't run this company successfully if I have to be concerned about the people I trust going off in their own direction, doing things that aren't conducive to the vision I have for my business. I need to trust you fully."

Frederick nodded his head vehemently. "Cat, of course you can trust me. I'd never…"

She laughed. "I know and I do, which is why I didn't fire you. We've been friends for longer than we've been business associates. And I have great respect for your opinion. I hope you know how much you mean to me."

Every muscle in Frederick's body was smiling brightly. "So what's next?" he asked, the lines in his face finally relaxing.

She paused, reflecting on his question. As a company they were as ready as they were ever going to be. And if Noah's investigation didn't dig anything else up, she fathomed the stock release would go smoothly. She suddenly thought about the highly publicized event. She'd been invited to stand behind the New York Stock Exchange podium to push the button that signaled the bells that would announce the opening of the trading day. It was an honor and would symbolize a lifetime of achievement. She'd been dreaming of that moment since the first Fly High plane took flight.

"On Monday I want you with me when the bells ring," she finally said. "You should be there."

Frederick sat upright, understanding washing over his expression. He nodded, excitement playing on his face. "Of course, Cat. Thank you."

"Good. I'll arrange for car service to take us. Noah and I will be leaving from here. We need to be there by nine o'clock."

"Noah?"

Catherine nodded. She turned to jot some notes

onto a yellow lined notepad. "Yes. I anticipate…" she started.

Frederick snapped, cutting off her words abruptly. "Why is Noah going to be there?"

Catherine was taken aback by the rage that flashed across Frederick's face. His eyes were bulging and his face was flushed a deep hue of ruby red. He was clenching his teeth so tightly that every blood vessel in his face and neck was engorged. For a brief moment she imagined that if he could have, he would have hit her, his fists clenched like locked vises at his sides.

She took a deep breath and held it as she pushed herself back from the table. She turned her entire body to face him.

"Noah will be there because I want him there. He will be there to support me just like you will."

"So are you two an item now?" Frederick's eyes were now thin slits, his gaze narrowed tightly.

She met the look he was giving her with one of her own. "Noah is very important to me. Whatever the relationship is between us is no one's business but ours."

"We have a strict no-fraternization policy, Cat! Do you remember that? How is that going to look to our other employees?"

Catherine continued to eye him as intensely as he was eyeing her. His question was one that she and Noah had both asked themselves. Noah's answer had surprised her, and she'd been replaying the conversation over in her head since he'd left her that morning.

The morning sun had just risen in a picture-perfect sky. Catherine had stretched her naked body against his, relishing the warmth of his skin against her own. It felt good to wake up next to him, and she imagined that going back to a life without Noah there would truly break her heart.

There was something remarkable growing between them. Something mesmerizing and consuming. She found herself craving him like she'd never craved anything before. It was intoxicating and she felt as if it were the sweetest addiction imaginable. But she was reluctant to label it because that four-letter word had always scared her. Love wasn't something she ever imagined for herself, not even in passing.

Noah must have sensed her musings as he snuggled closer against her, nuzzling his face into her hair. He had gently kissed the back of her neck as he murmured good morning against her ear. His breath was hot against her skin and the sensation caused a shiver to course through her body.

"I was dreaming about you," he'd whispered softly.

She'd smiled into the pillow. "Hmm. Good dreams, I hope."

He'd nodded. "Really good dreams. I dreamed you married me."

Catherine had then rolled in his arms, turning her body to face him. "Really?"

"You married me and we made beautiful babies and lived in Salt Lake City and we were incredibly happy."

His comment had surprised her. "Marriage?"

Noah had laughed. "You do know what that is, right?"

She'd pushed her palm against his bare chest. "Don't be silly. I just… Well…I…" she stammered, suddenly at a loss for words.

"We can't keep our relationship a secret forever," Noah said. "And at some point it's going to be a problem with my employment. So you really need to think about marrying me. If we get married then no one can say anything about you sleeping around with one of your employees. And people wouldn't think twice about your husband working for your business."

Catherine had laughed. "We must both still be dreaming," she'd said softly.

Noah had cupped his hand around her face, tilting her gaze to his. "Think about it, Cat. Because I'm going to ask you proper. In the very near future I'm going to get down on one knee with a ring in hand and I'm going to ask you to be my wife. And you'll need to have an answer for me."

"But…"

He pressed his index fingers to her lips, stalling her doubts. "No buts. Just give it some thought."

She'd been thinking about it ever since. Noah would be expecting an answer from her and she instinctively knew that her answer wasn't going to sit well with Frederick.

She changed the subject. "Frederick, my friend,

you worry too much. Don't make this something it doesn't need to be."

Before he could respond Marvin burst through the door. "Sorry to interrupt but they're evacuating the building. There's been a bomb threat!"

Noah was finding it increasingly difficult to concentrate on the task at hand. Despite his best efforts, his mind kept drifting back to thoughts of Catherine. They'd spent the past few days having serious conversations about their relationship. Waking up that morning, he'd been thinking about marriage and he'd said so, the prospect surprising them both.

What was growing between them had taken on a life of its own. It had happened faster than either of them could have ever imagined and it wasn't going away. One day they'd been high school acquaintances reconnecting and the next day neither of them could imagine a future without each other. On one hand it all made perfect sense. On the other it was the craziest thing he had ever experienced. But the more he thought about the two of them together, the more certain he was that he had fallen head over heels in love with Catherine Moore. He loved her. That scared him and made his heart sing in the same breath. The sudden intensity of emotions they were both feeling felt as natural to him as breathing but he knew he needed to take a step back and re-evaluate what was going on. The element of fear that came with commitment had him second-guessing what he was most certain about and it was a necessary occurrence. His pragmatic nature wouldn't allow for anything less.

He deeply sighed as the office administrator dropped a stack of folders onto the makeshift desk where he'd been working. He'd been at it for hours, confirming a series of numbers on a computer-generated spreadsheet. The reports should have corresponded with each other but one had been edited, and then a second, throwing all the numbers off. The pilot hours and the plane's mileage logs didn't match and they should have. Noah had needed the originals to confirm why.

He looked up at the woman who was assisting him. "These two pilots, Paul Contreras and Michael Thames, are they not employees of Fly High?"

The buxom blonde shook her head. "No, sir, they're both independent contractors. We use them when our regular pilots are unavailable."

"Who makes that call?"

"Usually Mr. Ross."

"Do me a favor, please, and pull the employee records for the regular pilots."

The woman nodded, her smile filling her face. "Yes, sir, Mr. Stallion."

Noah watched as the woman walked out of the room, her thin hips shimmying from side to side. She tossed him a look over her shoulder, invitation in her eyes. Noah ignored the implementation, turning his attention back to his papers.

His cell phone suddenly rang, vibrating against

the tabletop. Answering it, he leaned back in his seat. "Hello?"

"Noah Stallion?"

"Speaking."

"Hey, man, it's Kendrick Boudreaux. How are you?"

"Kendrick, hello. I really appreciate you giving me a call."

"No big deal. My man John said you needed some help."

Noah smiled into the receiver. When he'd reached out to his first cousin he hadn't expected the familial connection that would have put him in contact with a bona fide government agent. But John's brother-in-law, Kendrick Boudreaux, worked for the Secret Service and from everything his Dallas cousins had shared, he'd participated in a number of high-level, covert missions before marrying his new wife Vanessa. Noah had figured if anyone could point him in the right direction, Kendrick could.

"I hate to be a bother but I could really use a hand," Noah said, explaining what he needed and why.

Kendrick listened intently. Noah could hear him jotting down notes on his end of the line. "And what do you think is going on?" he asked.

Noah sighed. "I'm no rocket scientist but calculating the distance those planes traveled based on the actual mileage and not the mileage that was reported, the only place any of them could have gone was across the border into Mexico and back. I could be wrong but it's the only thing that makes sense. The looming question is why? I don't have the connections or the resources on that end to try and figure it out."

"Well, I have a few favors I can call in. Let me see what I can dig up."

"I would really appreciate that."

"And do you think the email threats are connected? Or do you have two separate problems?"

"I want to say they're one and the same but I could be wrong."

"Can you forward all of those emails to me?" Kendrick asked. "I have a crackerjack team of internet specialists who can track down an IP address like they're going to their mother's house."

Noah laughed. "I sure can. Consider them on the way."

"And give me a few hours to see what I can dig up on your plane problem. I'll give you a call as soon as I have some answers."

"Man, I can't tell you how much I appreciate your help. I'll owe you big-time."

"Don't sweat it, bro. It's what family does, and you know that Stallion-Boudreaux connection runs deep."

"I think I heard that somewhere!" Noah laughed.

"You can trust it. I know I do," Kendrick said as he disconnected the call.

The return call from Kendrick came minutes before Noah's plane was preparing to take off. Their conversation was extensive, Noah not liking anything he had heard. The situation was even worse than he'd imagined.

"There will be a federal investigation," Kendrick was saying. "But I'll do everything I can to keep it on the low."

"How long do I have?" Noah questioned. "I need to get to Catherine. I'm flying back to New York as we speak. But I don't want her blindsided, especially since the company goes public on Monday."

"I'm flying into the city tonight. More than likely we will execute a warrant tomorrow morning. That's probably the best I'm going to be able to do. But I'm also going to need you to keep the lid on this. We can't risk them finding out that we're onto them. If they run we could lose this whole case."

Noah extended his appreciation, the two men agreeing to speak again once Kendrick landed in New York. He disconnected the call and signaled the pilot to take off. His mind was racing. He'd gone looking for something and what he'd found was bigger than he could have fathomed. It was dark and dirty and he didn't need a federal investigation to tell him that it started and stopped at Frederick's door. Catherine was going to be devastated.

His anxiety was raging. His knee shook with a vengeance. His first priority was to protect Catherine, though Catherine was going to want to protect Fly High. Doing both successfully would be a test of Noah's business acumen. He couldn't help but think that solving a double murder might have been easier.

Noah wasn't surprised to find the corporate headquarters empty when he finally found his way back to downtown Manhattan. The moment they'd landed and he'd been able to turn his cell phone back on, a lengthy list of text and voice messages welcomed his arrival. He and Catherine had only hung up after she'd been called back for more questioning, investigators ensuring the bomb threat had been a cruel prank and nothing more.

Bishop stood behind the reception desk and a half-dozen NYPD officers loitered in the lobby. Dismay washed over Noah's face as he looked toward the police and back to his friend.

Bishop's head nodded anxiously in his direction. "Miss Cat is expecting you, Mr. Stallion. She's in the boardroom. I think there's a detective still there with her and Mr. Ross."

He nodded his head. "Is someone doing rounds?"

"That new boy, Jimmy, and one of them police officers are walking around now. I'll do the next shift myself."

Noah sighed. "Call me when you're ready, Mr. Bishop. I'd like to walk the floors with you."

Bishop grinned. "Yes, sir."

Noah nodded at the officers who all turned to stare as he waited for the elevators to take him up to the twelfth floor. It was only a few minutes later when he stepped into the company boardroom. Catherine sat at the head of the table, a detective sitting in the seat beside her. Frederick stood, his hand gently caressing Catherine's back and shoulder in a gesture of comfort. Noah felt himself bristle as he struggled to keep the emotion void from his face. It took everything he had not to cross the room and snatch the smirk from Frederick's lips. The two men locked eyes and held the stare far longer than necessary.

Catherine didn't miss the rise of tension that suddenly flooded the room. "Noah, I'm glad you're back," she said, rising from her seat and rushing to his side. She stopped short of throwing her body into his arms, but he could see the fright and frustration that pierced her dark eyes. She paused and took a deep breath as he reached for her hands and held them between his own.

His smile was slight but endearing. "Are you okay?" he asked, his voice a loud whisper.

"Yes." She nodded. "I am now." She took another deep breath. "Noah Stallion, this is Detective Joe Locke," she said as she gestured in the police officer's direction. "Detective Locke, this is Noah Stallion. He's our vice president of security."

The two men shook hands.

"It's a pleasure," Noah said. "I'm sorry I couldn't get back here sooner. Do we know anything yet?"

The detective shook his fire-engine-red hair. "Our bomb squad has cleared the building and they didn't find anything. Right now we're thinking it was just a hoax. The call came in from a disposable phone so we're unable to trace it. But it was probably someone's kid playing games. I don't think you have anything real to be worried about."

"I beg to differ," Frederick suddenly chimed in. "I think we need to be very worried. Did you not hear me when I said that Ms. Moore's life had been previously threatened? In fact," he continued, turning his attention toward Noah, "had you been here you would have known that she received more email messages today and this time she was threatened with physical harm."

Noah tossed Catherine a quick look. She was chewing anxiously on her bottom lip, sadness floating in her gaze.

"We can look into that," the detective said. "Make sure my office gets copies of those messages."

"We appreciate that, Detective, but I can assure you it's being handled," Noah said emphatically as he turned to stare at Frederick.

The two men locked gazes both eyeing the other with distaste. Catherine's eyes shifted back and forth between the two. She sensed that whatever ill will the two were harboring wasn't going to go away anytime soon.

Noah's deep voice interrupted her thoughts. "Detective, if we can speak privately, please?" He gestured for the man to follow him as he headed back toward the door.

Detective Locke extended his goodbyes to Catherine and Frederick and made his exit.

Once the door was closed, Frederick's anger seethed. "I don't know how he can believe that you aren't in harm's way."

She shook her head. "If Noah says he has it handled, then I trust him. If he's not worried, you shouldn't be. You hired him because he's good, or did you forget that?"

"No, I didn't forget. That's why I am worried. Noah was good but I can't help but question whether or not your relationship with him is distracting him from his responsibilities."

Frederick's comment was snarky and uncalled for, Catherine thought. Annoyance painted her expression. She shifted the conversation back to the tasks at hand. "I need you to make sure this doesn't hit the news feeds. And if it does we need to get on top of the story with a press statement. So do your job, please, and let me worry about Noah."

"If I'm being honest, I have questions about your judgment, as well," Frederick snapped, his tone edged in barbed wire.

Catherine narrowed her gaze as she eyed him. There was an awkward silence between the two. She finally nodded her head slightly before responding.

"Frederick, I'm going to assume that you're tired, and with everything that has happened you aren't thinking clearly. But so there are no further misunderstandings, don't think that I'm okay with you speaking to me that way because I'm not. And since I've warned you once before, please trust that this will be the last time. Right now I've got way too much on my mind to deal with your foolishness. But I will deal with it." She let out a low sigh before she continued.

"Handle the media, get a good night's sleep and come back tomorrow like you want to continue to be employed by this company. If you can't handle that I'll accept your resignation now."

Frederick took a step toward her, contrition flooding his expression. "Cat, I'm sorry, I didn't…"

"Good night, Frederick," she said, cutting him off.

As she turned to sit, Noah moved back into the room. He didn't miss the sudden strain that seemed to paint the four walls. "Are you here in the morning?" he asked, directing his question at Frederick.

The man nodded. "Of course. Catherine needs me, and I would never leave her hanging." He tossed her a quick look.

"I need to speak to you both about my trip," Noah said.

"Exactly where is it you went, anyway?" Frederick asked.

Noah barely shrugged his shoulders as his eyes met the look Catherine was giving him. He didn't bother to answer the question. "We'll talk in the morning," he said, his gaze still locked on Catherine's face.

He gave Frederick a dismissive glance, his eyes not lingering long enough to focus. "Catherine, I want to do rounds with Mr. Bishop. It shouldn't take too long."

She nodded. "I'll be in my office when you're done," she said, returning her attention to the stream of paperwork before her.

Both men retreated from the room at the same time. Out in the hallway, Frederick turned abruptly, waving an index finger in Noah's face.

"I don't know what kind of games you're playing, Stallion but…"

Noah's movement was unexpected as he took a quick step in the other man's direction, pushing him hard against the wall. He'd just drawn back his arm, his fist raised, when Bishop interrupted the moment.

"Everything okay here, son?"

Noah's face was rigid, his muscles taut, his teeth clenched tightly. Anger flooded his spirit, and he was suddenly stunned by it. He stepped back, dropping his arm down to his side, his hand still clenched in a tight ball. He cleared his throat. "Yes, sir," he finally said. "We're good."

Frederick's eyes were wide, something like fear seeping from his stare. Without saying a word, he pushed his way past Noah, hurrying down the hall and out of sight.

Chapter 11

Since leaving the office, Noah and Catherine had barely spoken to each other, both seemingly lost in their own thoughts. Without giving it a second thought, Catherine instructed the driver to take them to the Blue Ribbon Sushi Bar and Grill. The Columbus Circle restaurant was one of her favorites and she'd promised to take Noah since he'd first arrived in New York. Needing someplace familiar to ease her nerves, she didn't bother to ask if he was interested in going or not, just hoping he wouldn't be disappointed by her choice.

After being seated, she ordered a bottle of wine, and when he deferred the menu choices to her, she added enough platters of sushi and sashimi to feed a small army.

Noah eyed her with a raised brow as she threw back her first glass of wine, quickly refilling it with her second. "You look like you need to talk," he said. He reached for the bottle and filled his own glass.

Catherine met his gaze, tears teasing her eyes. "Why is this happening? I am this close—" she gestured with her thumb and forefinger "—to seeing one of my biggest dreams accomplished and I suddenly feel like all my hard work is about to blow up into pieces." She sighed deeply.

"I'm sorry. I know it's a lot to deal with but you're going to be fine, Cat. Baby, you're one of the strongest women I know. No matter what happens, you'll turn this around. And I'll be right there with you. You won't have to face any of this alone."

She nodded. A single tear escaped past her lashes. She swiped at her face with the back of her left hand as she reached for his hand with her right. They entwined their fingers tightly together. Catherine held on to his as if letting go was not an option.

"So," Noah started, "you still haven't told me everything that happened today."

She shrugged. "There's really not much else to tell. You got all the details about the bomb threat, and Frederick spilled the news about the email threats."

Noah nodded. "I read them."

She shook her head. "I don't know who would want to hurt me."

"What do you know about Frederick?" Noah asked, his tone hardening.

She eyed him curiously. "Frederick? Why would

you ask me…?" Her voice faded, her words failing as she noted the look on Noah's face.

"Because I don't trust him and I think his obsession with you isn't healthy."

"Now you sound like Marvin."

"Marvin told me he had concerns about him also."

"I think Marvin overreacts. You, too. Frederick and I have always been good friends. I've never had any reason to doubt him. He's been good for the business, so why wouldn't I trust him?"

Noah nodded. This time he poured a second glass of wine, taking a large swallow. "I think Frederick is responsible for the emails. I think he's been trying to scare you on purpose so that you would depend on him more."

Catherine's look was incredulous. "That's ridiculous. He wouldn't…" She paused while her eyes skated rapidly from side to side. "Do you really think he would do that to me?"

"Everything I uncovered in Texas says he's good for it."

She slowly shook her head. "I don't believe this."

"I called in a favor from a friend with the Secret Service. Everything he uncovered points to Frederick. But there's more and it's worse."

Catherine fell back against her seat. From the expression on his face she was suddenly afraid to ask what he'd learned. She pulled a hand to her mouth, her anxiety level quickly rising. "Do I need to call my attorneys?" she questioned.

Noah blew a deep breath. "I've already spoken to them. The team will meet with us in the morning."

"It's that bad?"

Noah nodded. "My friend Kendrick says that the feds will try to keep it as quiet as they can. But it's not good, Cat, and you need to be prepared."

"What is it?" She leaned forward in her seat.

For the next thirty minutes, Noah repeated everything Kendrick Boudreaux had relayed to him. He told her how they suspected her planes were being used to smuggle contraband back and forth across the Mexican border. He explained how pilots Frederick had contracted were known traffickers wanted by the FBI. He informed her that aircraft she had believed grounded for repairs were, in fact, being used to transport young women and girls for the purpose of prostitution. The affront list was lengthy. By the time Noah was done Catherine sat sobbing over her sushi, shock registering over her entire body.

Noah tossed his cloth napkin to the table, sliding out of the booth they sat in. He moved to her side of the table and sat next to her, wrapping his arms around her shoulders. He held her close as she clutched the front of his shirt, her tears staining the starched fabric. He held her until her sobs shifted to a low sniffle.

"I'm going to kill him. In fact, the minute I leave here, I'm going to go tell him exactly what I think about him," she snapped. "And then I'm going to wring his neck!"

"You can't."

"What do you mean I can't? Because I have every intention of telling him what a lowlife piece of scum he is."

Noah nodded. "I understand how you feel, Cat, but until Kendrick, the FBI and the CIA execute their plan tomorrow we can't let on that we know anything. We can't afford to spook him or any of the people he might be associated with."

Catherine rolled her eyes. Her jaw tightened with rage. "Fine," she said, sounding only somewhat convincing. "But keep him away from me tomorrow. Until they come for him, keep him as far from me as you can."

"There's one more thing," Noah said, meeting her eyes evenly. "They are going to want to talk to you tomorrow. To see if you had any prior knowledge of what was going on."

Her gaze narrowed substantially. "Why does that sound so ominous?"

"Your attorney will be with you and he'll advise you all the way. Just answer their questions honestly and there shouldn't be any problems."

"Why are you saying that like they think I had something to do with all this mess?"

"I'm saying that the investigation into Fly High and its management team is just beginning. Everyone is a suspect."

Catherine shook her head, anger replacing the hurt that she'd been feeling. "I don't deserve this," she said, reaching for the wine bottle. "I don't deserve this and I will not let Frederick and whatever he screwed up ruin what I've worked all these years to build!"

Neither Noah nor Catherine could sleep. Both tossed and turned for most of the night. At some ungodly hour in the early part of the morning, Noah threw his legs off the side of the mattress and rose from the bed. Catherine was nowhere to be found. He walked through each room of the home looking for her. He checked his cell phone but there were no new messages. He dialed her number, but she didn't answer his call and there was no note anywhere in sight. He could only begin to imagine where she'd disappeared.

Moving to stare out the expanse of windows, he didn't even know where to begin to look for her. New York was her city, not his, and she could have been anywhere. He thought for a brief moment before sending her a quick text message. Then he called the security office at Fly High. Bishop answered on the second ring.

"Mr. Bishop, it's Noah Stallion. I was looking for Cat. Is she in her office by chance?"

"No. No, sir. I haven't seen her since you two left earlier. Nothing's wrong, is there?"

Noah could almost see the old man shaking his head with concern. "No, sir, Mr. Bishop. She's just anxious about the IPO offering next week."

"That little girl doesn't get enough rest. You need to help her get some rest."

"I'm trying, sir. I really am."

The old man said something else but Noah didn't hear him, the sound of the front door opening and then closing catching his attention. "Mr. Bishop, I found her. Thank you. I'm sure I'll see you before your shift ends," he said as he disconnected the call.

He called her name. "Are you okay?"

Catherine moved into the room where he stood. She was dressed in a black sweat suit, the hood pulled up over her head. Her eyes were swollen from crying and her cheeks were tinged red. She met his stare and watched as the concern lifted off his shoulders. She suddenly felt horrible for having let him worry about her.

"Hey, I'm sorry. I should have left you a note."

Noah nodded. "No problem. You're a big girl. I know you can take care of yourself."

She shrugged her narrow shoulders. "Twenty-four hours ago I would have agreed with you."

He smiled. "I was worried but only because I know you're worried. I hate to see you so stressed."

She took a deep breath. "I might be going to jail for something I didn't do. I have every reason to be stressed."

"You won't be going to jail, Cat."

"You don't know that, Noah. You don't know what's going to happen with this investigation. Because neither one of us knows exactly what Frederick has or hasn't done. And as the president and CEO of this company I should have known what was going on with my business. The fact that something was going on under my watch doesn't look good. Isn't that right?"

Noah took a deep breath. "You're right about one thing. We don't know what Frederick has done. But we do know that you haven't done anything wrong. And I know that I'm not going to let anything happen to you. That I promise you."

"How can you promise me that?"

A pregnant pause swelled full and thick between them before Noah finally spoke again. "Because I love you. I love you, Cat, and I will do whatever I have to do to protect you."

He moved in her direction, taking four quick steps to her side. Catherine lifted her gaze to stare into his. The look he was giving her was soul deep, the connection between them fraught with a feeling of contentment she'd never known before. She stepped into his outstretched arms, the mettle of her spirit feeling like it had found its way home.

"I love you, baby," Noah said as he tightened his embrace. "I love you very much."

Catherine nestled herself closer against him, looping her arms around his back. She snuggled her face against his chest. "I love you, too, Noah Stallion. I love you more than you know."

Kendrick Boudreaux and a team of federal agents were waiting in the Fly High lobby when Catherine and Noah entered the building. Catherine tensed, and Noah pressed a hand to the small of her back, his touch easing the strain that pulled at her spirit. Noah made the introductions.

"Thank you for coming, Agent Boudreaux," she said. "Whatever you need from me, just ask. You can trust that everyone here will be completely transparent."

Kendrick nodded. "We appreciate that. Your legal team is already talking with two of our agents. I know they have some questions for you but first I need to ensure that you understand your rights," he said.

Catherine nodded. "I do. My attorney briefed me earlier."

"We just want to make sure we have all the facts, Ms. Moore."

"Please, Noah said you two are almost like family. You can call me Cat."

Kendrick smiled. "I don't want you to worry, Cat. We're going to get this cleared up and be out of your way before you know it."

She smiled, desperately wanting to believe the man.

Kendrick tossed a quick glance down to his wristwatch. "What time do you expect Mr. Ross?" he asked.

"He should be here any minute now," Noah answered.

"You two should go on up to the conference room then," Kendrick said. "We'll handle it all from here."

It was almost an hour later before Frederick marched into the conference room, escorted by Kendrick and two other well-dressed agents. He looked flustered, clearly miffed by what was going on. His gaze snapped left and then right before resting on Catherine's face. She met his stare, glaring in his direction before shifting her eyes away. She nodded her head at the man interrogating her, answering whatever question it was that he had just asked.

"Would someone please tell me what's going on?" Frederick snapped. "Cathcrine? Why are there federal agents crawling through the building?"

Catherine suddenly jumped from her seat, her index finger waving vehemently as her body snapped toward him. She shouted, "Because you and your dirty dealings brought them to my door! That's why they're here. They're here to clear my name and the name of my company and until that happens we will welcome them with open arms."

Noah moved between the two, using his body to block her view of the man. He could only imagine what might happen if Frederick got too close to her, getting a visual of Catherine tearing the man's eyes out. Just the sight of him had her raging.

Frederick bristled. The color drained from his face, and he broke out into a cold sweat. He opened his mouth to speak then closed it, saying nothing at all.

Kendrick interjected, gesturing toward Catherine to retake her seat. "Mr. Ross, please, if you'll just take a seat. We have a few questions for you."

Frederick dropped into a cushioned chair. He was visibly shaking, his hands quivering as he clutched them together in his lap. He stole another glance toward Catherine out of the corner of his eye.

"Mr. Ross, we found a laptop computer locked in the lower drawer of your desk. Is that a personal computer or a business computer, sir?"

"You were in my desk?"

"Is it company property, sir, or personal property?"

"It's…umm…well…it's…" he stammered.

Kendrick repeated the question, his voice rising slightly.

"It belongs to Fly High," Frederick finally muttered.

Kendrick nodded. "Does anyone else have a key to your desk besides you, sir?"

Frederick shrugged. "I don't know. I don't think… Why are you asking me these questions?"

Kendrick smiled. "We're just trying to get to the bottom of some things, sir. Are you the only one with access to that laptop, Mr. Ross?"

Frederick's gaze skated across the faces staring back at him. "I need to speak with our attorneys," he said.

Kendrick nodded. "Are you invoking your right to council, Mr. Ross?"

He nodded. "It's my right," he said emphatically.

"Yes, it is," Kendrick said.

He tilted his head at one of the other agents, his eyebrows raised. The other man crossed the room, seeming to pull a pair of handcuffs out of thin air. Frederick's eyes widened.

"Mr. Ross, you are under arrest," Kendrick said. "You've been read your rights and we'll let the record show you've requested legal representation."

Frederick sputtered. "I… But…Catherine…please!"

Catherine shook her head, folding her arms across her chest. Her face was blank, no hint of emotion painting her expression.

The company's senior attorney rose from her seat beside Catherine. She was a tall, leggy brunette who bore an amazing resemblance to Angelina Jolie. She moved to Frederick's side. "Mr. Ross, have your attorney contact me, please. I'll need to discuss the terms of your dismissal."

"My dismissal?"

"Fly High has optioned the morals clause in your employment contract, finding you in violation. Your employment has subsequently been terminated without prejudice."

Before Frederick could respond, the FBI agent pushed him toward the door and out of the room.

Catherine shook her head, relief finally seeping from her eyes.

Kendrick nodded at Noah, a wide smile on his face. "Your girl has some fire in her." He chuckled softly. "I hate to think what might have happened if she'd gotten her hands on him."

Noah laughed with him. "You don't know the half of it," he whispered back.

Catherine tossed both men a harsh look, finding nothing at all to laugh about. "What was the deal with the computer you asked him about?" she asked, spinning around in her seat.

"It's the computer that was used to send you threatening messages," Kendrick answered.

Disbelief washed over her expression. "He was behind that? You're kidding me, right?"

Kendrick shook his head. "Sorry."

Catherine rubbed at her eyes with both hands. The man across the table from her resumed his questioning of more things that she had no knowledge of. It was about three hours later when the agents finally packed their belongings. Fly High attorneys had turned over all relevant documents that were needed to support the case against Frederick.

Relief came in abundance when Kendrick shook her hand, assuring her that she had nothing to worry about and wishing her much success with taking her company public.

"I'm sure we'll have more questions for you, Cat, but Mr. Ross wasn't as thorough about covering his tracks as he had thought. We won't have any problems building a case against him. Your cooperation has been essential and I'm confident that we'll have no issues showing that he manipulated you and your company for his own personal gain."

Catherine nodded. "What about the threatening emails? Why did he do that?"

Noah answered that question. "I think he figured that if he staged and controlled the threats then he could make himself look good when they magically went away."

"That man's delusional."

Kendrick and Noah exchanged an all-knowing look between them.

Noah shrugged. "Being in love can make a man crazy."

"And if he's already crazy it will make him psychotic," Kendrick added.

Catherine looked from one to the other. She didn't bother to respond, turning her attention instead to Noah. "What now?"

Noah smiled, an air of mischief suddenly shimmering in his eyes.

Chapter 12

They'd been in the air for over an hour, and Catherine still had more questions than she did answers. Their day had started early and it didn't look like it was going to end anytime soon.

Noah had been right by her side when she'd rung the bell to announce that the stock market had officially opened. Then she'd become obsessed with the ticker. For some the flashing series of letters, arrows and numbers scrolling across the screen was puzzling but for Catherine that cryptic script was everything she had been dreaming about. It was her lifeline, keeping her abreast of market sentiment. It had been her intentions to follow each tick, every up and down movement in the price of the security until the closing bell rang. But Noah hadn't allowed it.

After lunch and the last celebratory toast Noah had escorted her to a waiting car and then to the airport. After a heated argument he'd taken her cell phone and her iPad, leaving her technologically challenged, and she was still angry about it, desperate to see where they were on the NASDAQ.

She cut her eye at him, becoming even more annoyed by the smug expression on his face. She then directed her gaze back to the view outside, marveling at the cushion of clouds they were floating on. She let out a heavy gust of breath past her glossed lips.

Noah laughed heartily.

"What?" she snapped, her head whipping around to glare at him.

"You and that poor attitude of yours," he said.

Catherine prickled. "My attitude?"

He nodded. "Yes, and I'm putting you on notice right now that if you don't adjust it and quick, I won't have any problem adjusting it for you."

Her eyes widened, her mouth falling open. "I beg your pardon!"

Noah shifted forward in his seat. "I firmly believe in corporal punishment. I won't have any problems spanking that delectable backside of yours."

Catherine stared at him then suddenly burst out laughing. "Spank me? I wish you would!" she quipped.

Noah's smirk widened. "Be careful what you wish for," he said, his tone low and seductive. "I would love to palm that bare bottom." Amusement danced in the look he was giving her.

Catherine laughed again, a hint of nervousness teasing her senses. "You're a fool, Noah Stallion!"

He leaned forward and kissed her lips. "A fool in love," he said.

She kissed him back. "Keep working that Stallion magic and I might not stay mad at you."

"I don't know why you're mad at all."

She tossed up her hands in frustration. "You've cut me off from everything! How can you not know?"

"You need to unwind. I didn't have any other choice."

"So can I have my devices back now?"

"No."

She rolled her eyes. "Then I'm going to stay mad. You know I want to check the stock prices and see how we're doing."

"You don't need to check. The underwriters said they would send you an update at the end of the day. And they will."

"But..."

"But nothing. You can't single-handedly control the stock market and you need to stop trying. It's going to be fine. You just need to let it go and relax."

Her eyes rolled into the back of her head once again. "Then I'm staying mad."

He gave her a quick shrug of his broad shoulders. "Like I said, I can fix that attitude of yours." He rubbed his palms together, still grinning at her.

Catherine stared back at him, fighting not to laugh at his silliness. She changed the subject. "Can you at least tell me where we're going?" she questioned.

Noah nodded. "Paris."

"France?"

"That's where Paris is, Ms. Moore." He tilted his head just so as he looked at her.

Her face flushed with color. "I've never been to Paris," she said softly.

Noah looked surprised. "Really? I don't know why I thought…"

She shook her head. "I always imagined that the first time I went to Paris that it would be on my honeymoon or anniversary."

"I hope you're not disappointed."

Catherine smiled. "How could I be disappointed about seeing Paris with the man I love?"

Noah's smile was sugar sweet as he reached for her hand and held it, gently squeezing her fingers beneath his own.

"So, why are we going to Paris, France?" she asked.

"It's Fashion Week and I wanted you to meet my family."

Confusion washed over her expression and it made him laugh.

"My sister Natalie is walking Paris Fashion Week and her husband is introducing his new fall clothing line. The entire Stallion clan will be there to support them. I thought it would be nice if we were there, too."

Catherine nodded, allowing what Noah told her to settle into her head. A few minutes later she held up her hand, having one last question to ask him.

"Yes?" Noah smiled.

"Who owns this plane? Because it's not one of mine."

* * *

After another hour of lighthearted banter, Catherine was still testy, and Noah continued to tease her. Finally, tired of trying to cajole him into giving her electronics back to her, she pulled her body across the leather seats and laid her head in Noah's lap, drifting off into a deep sleep.

Noah drew his hand over her hair, his fingers gently tracing her profile. It felt good to see her finally relax. After everything that had happened Noah realized that he would have to take a few drastic measures in order to get her to step back and regroup.

After their Friday-morning encounter with the federal authorities, she'd been beside herself with anxiety and nothing seemed to soothe her shattered nerves. Despite her best efforts to resume her business-as-usual attitude there had been nothing familiar or normal about what she was feeling. Nothing Noah had said or done had moved her back to a state of normalcy.

His sister's late-night call to ask yet again if he could come to Paris for her runway show had been all the convincing he'd needed. His cousins John and Matthew Stallion had arranged their transportation, sending the Stallion family jet to retrieve them. Refusing Catherine access to her phone and the internet had been the least of his concerns, knowing that nothing else would have helped him achieve his goal.

Now they were a few short hours from landing. He'd already planned an early-morning meal with his family, and sometime before the week was finished he would be asking her to marry him atop the Eiffel Tower. With much help from his family and friends he could only hope and pray that his plans would come together before Catherine would be kicking and screaming to get back to the Fly High headquarters.

He smiled down at her. It was the first time in days that she actually looked at peace. Frederick's betrayal had devastated her. She had genuinely considered him her friend and she had never wanted to believe that he could actually cause her pain. She didn't have to tell him how hurt she was because she wore it over her spirit, the weight so heavy that he could literally see it stealing every ounce of her joy when it crossed her thoughts. Noah knew it would take time and prayer to move her past that wealth of pain.

She shifted against him, slipping a hand beneath her head as she made herself more comfortable. Her fingers teased the length of his manhood and the grazing of her nails moved him to smile, a current of electricity shooting through his groin.

Noah took a deep breath and then another, holding the air in his lungs until it burned, distracting him from the rise of nature that strained for attention. He dropped his hand against the curve of her waist, allowing his palm to gently tease the round of her buttocks. He tapped the sumptuous flesh gently and drifted off to sleep.

Catherine woke to the low roar of jet engines and Noah snoring lightly. He'd fallen slightly to the side, his bent elbow and hand supporting his head. She nuzzled herself closer against him, steeling herself against his firm frame.

The nap had been exactly what she had needed, suddenly feeling like all was well in the world. Relinquishing control to Noah had been difficult, but she liked how he'd commanded the reins, refusing to let her run roughshod over him.

Her father had wanted a son. Instead, he'd fathered a daughter. And Catherine had been a very prissy little girl. Papa Moore had no interest in her being a girly girl so she'd been programmed to master boy skills growing up. The patriarch had wanted to ensure she could take care of herself without the need to be dependent on a man to take care of her. That mindset had been to Catherine's benefit. She knew her way around a shotgun, could hold her own on a basketball court and she loved boxing. There wasn't anything with an engine or motor that she couldn't fix and she could scale a ladder with the best of them. Building a multi-million-dollar aviation business had been the cherry on top.

She wasn't used to having a man come to her rescue, but Noah seemed to do exactly that without reservation. Noah was the kind of man who wouldn't let her change a tire even though she knew how. She was discovering that she needed Noah just as much as she wanted him. But admitting that to him, and herself, didn't come without challenges. Relinquishing control wasn't easy despite his best efforts to help her do so.

Lifting her body upward, she nuzzled a path up

his torso, wrapping her arms around his waist as she laid her head on his chest. Noah let out a deep breath as he wrapped his arms around her, hugging her tightly. He pressed a kiss to the top of her head, his eyes still closed tightly. She relaxed into the rhythm of his breathing, the slow inhale and exhale like a sweet balm.

He held her, and she felt protected, feeling like nothing in the world could ever cause her harm. She soon fell back asleep, thoughts of Noah filling her dreams.

There was a car and driver waiting for them as they disembarked. In the distance the morning sun was just finding its spot in a cloud-filled sky. There was a distinct chill to the temperature and the promise of rain hung heavily in the air.

Noah greeted the man cheerily. *"Bonjour! Comment allez-vous?"*

The driver responded and the two enjoyed a brief conversation that Catherine found engaging. Noah's command of the French language came as a complete surprise to her.

"You speak French?"

He nodded. "Yes, and Italian," he answered.

"Wow!"

Noah laughed. "Why do you look so surprised?"

"I just didn't expect it."

"It's high school French. Back then I thought learning the romance languages would make me more attractive to the girls. I wanted to be suave and debonair."

She nodded. "It's definitely sexy as hell!" she exclaimed, a wry smile pulling at her mouth.

The eight-hour flight had afforded them a good night's sleep. The luxury shower had been a sheer delight, giving Catherine ideas for the expansion of their international fleet. Both showered and dressed, Noah was ready to show Catherine a full day of Parisian flair.

"So where are we off to?" Catherine asked, staring out the limousine window.

"Breakfast with my family right now." He looked at his watch. "And we're right on time."

Catherine suddenly looked like a deer in headlights. "Your family?"

He nodded. "What's wrong?"

She was frantically searching inside her leather backpack for her hairbrush and makeup bag. "What's wrong?" she quipped back. "Do you see how I look?"

He laughed. "You look beautiful!"

"I look like I just got off a plane after an eight-hour flight. What are they going to think?"

Noah laughed again. "Girl, please! You've bathed and you've used deodorant. As long as you don't smell I don't see what the problem is."

Catherine rolled her eyes as she checked her compact mirror. She looked refreshed, her complexion clear, her eyes bright. She opted not to add any more makeup. Instead, she pulled her hair into a loose bun atop her head. She shot Noah a look then laughed with him as he shook his head at her.

"I just want your family to like me," she exclaimed.

Noah leaned to kiss her lips. "My darling, they already love you."

The Stallion family resemblance ran deep. Catherine would have known Noah's family anywhere. All the men were tall, decadent drinks of water and the women Cover Girl pretty. They all had strong, chiseled features and their complexions were a range of Hershey's dark chocolate to black coffee with much, much cream.

The family was gathered for brunch at Nolita, the restaurant facing the Champs-Elysées complete with a view of the Eiffel Tower. It was ultracontemporary with a chic black-and-white interior and a trendy minimalist atmosphere. The menu was a melding of beautiful regional produce, Sicilian classics and unusual combinations that were sheer culinary magic. From the moment they stepped through the door, the aroma of rich, dark coffee and butter- and sugar-laced pastries intoxicated their senses.

Noah threw up his hand in greeting, the family cheering his name.

"You made it!" Natalie Stallion-Braddy shouted as she jumped to her feet when they entered. She rushed to throw her arms around her brother first and then Catherine. "It's so nice to meet you," she exclaimed as she pulled her into the room to meet the rest of the family.

Natalie tried to make the introductions easy, adding tidbits of information about each of her family to help Catherine remember who was who. She started with her husband Tinjin Braddy. Then there were Noah's twin brothers, Nathaniel and Nicholas, his sister Naomi, and his cousins and their spouses—John and Marah Stallion, Matthew and Katrina Stallion, Mark and Michelle Stallion, Luke and Joanne Stallion, Travis and Tierra Stallion and Phaedra Stallion Boudreaux and her husband, Mason.

"Katrina and Mason are sister and brother. And my husband, Tinjin, and Travis's wife, Tierra, are siblings," Natalie said, connecting as many of the dots as she could.

Everyone greeted Noah and her with hugs and kisses. They were all warm and welcoming and Catherine was made to feel right at home.

John Stallion gestured for the couple to take a seat. "Congratulations," he said. "Fly High has had two great trading days. You should be very proud."

Catherine's eyes widened.

Noah shook his head. "She's not allowed to check the numbers until we get back. This is a no-business business trip."

Catherine shook her fists feigning a temper tantrum. "He's going to drive me crazy!"

They all laughed.

"Well, we can assure you that you'll be pleased,"

Matthew interjected. "In fact, we couldn't resist making a sizeable investment ourselves."

"I've heard you're quite the business shark," Catherine said, eyeing John curiously. "You're not thinking about sneaking in to take my company, are you?"

"No." John laughed. "At least not today!"

"So when did you two get here?" Naomi asked, looking from Noah to Catherine and back.

"About an hour ago. We haven't even checked into the hotel yet."

"You'll love it!" Marah Stallion exclaimed. "It's one of my favorite places to stay."

"Do you get to Paris often?" Catherine asked.

Marah nodded. "Not as often as I'd like," she said, explaining that she and her husband were the proud adoptive parents of a rambunctious four-year-old. "Gabrielle is a handful."

"Do you want children?" Natalie asked, leaning closer to her.

"Don't answer that," Noah said, shaking his head.

Catherine laughed. "But…"

"I mean it. Do not give her any details about our relationship. Trust me when I tell you it's nothing but baby sister madness. They're crazy and they will make you crazy."

The Stallion men all laughed as Natalie and Phaedra shot each other a look.

"What's he trying to say?" Natalie questioned.

Phaedra shook her head. "I think he's being unreasonable. I have that problem with my big brothers every now and then, too."

Laughter was abundant as the family enjoyed their time together and they got to know her and she got to know them. Catherine was only slightly overwhelmed as she was pulled from one conversation to another.

"Now if you go to Brasserie Lipp for lunch, ask for a table on the ground floor. The ground floor is where the locals dine, and don't worry about your French. Most of the waiters speak perfect English," Tinjin said.

"If you go try the foie de veau," Natalie said. "It's divine."

Noah raised an eyebrow. "Calves liver?"

"It's really good. And after you can walk the side streets of the Left Bank where all the boutiques and shops are. There's the Rue de Bac, Rue de Sèvres, Rue des Saints-Pères, Rue de Grenelle, Rue du Four, Rue de Cherche-Midi, and the most exquisite lingerie in the world is at Sabbia Rosa. It's located on Rue des Saints-Pères. It's an amazing array of silk and lace like you've never seen before."

Naomi laughed. "She would know where the best shopping is."

Noah shook his head.

"So, what's the show schedule?" one of Noah's twin brothers asked.

Natalie nodded. "I'm walking Christian Dior tonight, Jean Paul Gaultier tomorrow, and of course, Tinmen on Thursday. We have tickets for everyone for every show. And of course you're invited to all the parties where all the pretty people will be."

"I'm here for the parties," Nathaniel said. "Beautiful models are right up my alley."

"I second that," Nicholas exclaimed.

"You better leave those women alone," Naomi said, skewering them with her expression.

"Do we have to do all the shows?" John questioned, looking to the other men for support. "I mean, we wouldn't miss Tinmen but I don't think I need to see what the other two designers have to offer. Marah picks out all my clothes now, anyway."

Marah rolled her eyes. "Really, John Stallion? This is the first time we've been to Paris together in ages and you want to go hang out with the men?"

"No, baby, I just don't want to go to a fashion show."

Mark nodded in agreement. "I was hoping we'd have some time to hit up the Christophe Pund classic car dealership. He's got some rare rides that I'd like to check out."

"Ooh, I want to do that, too," Michelle intoned.

Matthew laughed. "Sounds like someone is buying another car."

John shook his head. "You are not buying any more cars," he said, eyeing his brother.

Mark tossed Noah a look. "See how they treat me!"

They all laughed.

Tinjin interjected, "The girls are going to the Dior show. I thought we'd all head over to the Westminster Hotel to the Duke's Bar. It's this great little cigar club and it has an old English pub feel with live entertainment."

"I'm in," Luke said. He tossed his wife, Joanne, a wink of his eye.

"Well, I love all of you," Marah said, "but I fully intend to spend some quality married-people time with my husband since we don't have a child with us for a few days."

"I second that," Michelle chimed.

"I've got plans for my man, too," Katrina interjected.

Matthew laughed. "All right now."

Naomi tossed up her hands as if surrendering. "Too much information, people. Way too much information."

Chapter 13

Catherine and Noah both were in awe of the five-star boutique hotel that was modeled after an Italian opera house. Just minutes away from the Place Vendôme and the Palais Garnier, it sat in the heart of one of Paris's most beautiful districts. It boasted a magnificent smoking lounge and wine bar. It all made a striking first impression.

"And your cousin John owns this hotel?" she questioned, tossing Noah a look as she spun in a slow circle, taking it all in.

He nodded. "Mason, my cousin Phaedra's husband, actually built a successful hotel company that he sold to Stallion Enterprises a few years ago. That's actually how he and Phaedra first met. This was one of the original properties. I'm not quite sure how many hotels there are now but I know there's a lot."

Catherine nodded, still eyeing the exquisite surroundings. It was an exaltation of all her senses. The Stallion family had taken over the entire twenty-room property for the week, wanting their stay to feel like a family reunion. At the end of the week, in time for Tinjin and Natalie's runway event, they were going to be joined by the children and their nannies and other extended family members from New Orleans.

"Now, explain to me again how you're related to the Boudreauxs?"

Noah nodded and smiled. "Cousins by marriage. Mason and his sister Katrina married Stallions and then of course you've already met Kendrick. And they'll all be here later in the week because both families invested in Tinjin's company. They never miss any opportunity to support each other."

Noah opened the door to their suite. Inside, their luggage had already been delivered and someone had lit a fire in the brick fireplace. The space was decorated with heavy tapestries, sumptuous fabrics and elegant wooden furniture custom-designed by famed artist Jacques Garcia. An exquisite velvet sofa was nestled into an alcove, which looked like the perfect place to crawl up with a good book. There was an elegant marble bathroom and the toiletries were all by Hermès, the emblem of French luxury.

Like a kid in a candy shop, Catherine rushed from room to room, her excitement abundant. Her enthusiasm made Noah laugh. Catherine stepped out onto a charming private terrace that was shaded and landscaped with flowers. The atmosphere was intimate, romantic and sensuous. The design esthetic of the entire hotel combined the best of contemporary comfort with a lyrical romanticism. It was a haven of exoticism, quiet and dreams and she thought it absolutely magical. She felt her heart flutter with anticipation.

Stepping out onto the terrace with her, Noah studied the program his sister had left for them. There was a map, contact information for every imaginable need and a schedule of the planned events.

"I know this is your first trip to Paris so whatever you want to do is fine with me. From here we have some impressive neighbors. The royal Place Vendôme, which is a showcase for top luxury jewelers and the Second Empire Palais Garnier, home to the Paris Opera. If you want we can go for a walk and look around. And Tinjin said there are some art galleries and secret passages nearby. We're not far from the Palais-Royal gardens, too, which were built in the early seventeenth century. I've never seen them but I'm told they're beautiful."

Catherine shook her head. She turned to face him, a seductive stare blessing her face. She pulled the program from his hands and dropped it to a table adorned with a bouquet of white roses. She led him back inside and closed the glass doors behind them.

"We can do all of that," she said, "but why don't we save it for later. There's something else I'd like to do with you right now." Her voice was low, the rich alto tone a seductive breeze against his ear.

Rising desire seeped from Noah's eyes. "What did you have in mind, Ms. Moore?"

Catherine wrapped her arms around Noah's neck. Rising onto her toes, she kissed him, her mouth dancing eagerly over his. Her lips were heated. The kiss was intense, their tongues performing a slow, sensuous drag from one to the other.

The light of the fire lit the room and shadows from the flames danced over their faces. The soothing crackling of the firewood mixed with the soft lull of the opera *La bohème* playing through the speakers was all that could be heard.

Catherine was feeling toasty from the champagne they'd shared at brunch, and the look in Noah eyes melted her body into soft putty. He looked at her with such intensity, his love fueling his stare, that it made shivers course through her soul and take her breath away.

She guided his hands to her hips, stepping against him until her body was hugged tightly to his. He was panting softly, and she dropped her head to his chest to listen to the beat of his heart, the gentle thump beginning to sound like a heavy drum. Her knees suddenly felt weak. She imagined that if Noah had not been holding her in his arms, she would have dropped easily to the carpeted floor.

Noah's hand trailed over her curves, his fingers teasing each dip and valley. She took a step back as he fiddled with the buttons on her white blouse, slowly exposing inch after inch of warm brown flesh. He slipped the silk garment off her shoulders, tossing it to the floor behind her. He slowly caressed her skin, trailing his fingers across her stomach, along the curve of her breasts until he reached the curvature of her neck. He gently traced her profile, still staring into her eyes, and then he leaned forward to kiss her again.

Her lips parted in invitation, and his tongue tipped slowly in. His touch was exquisite and soft and warm. He tasted like the fresh berries he'd eaten. Catherine gasped softly, a low purr spilling past her lips. His mouth moved from her lips to her neck as he planted damp kisses against her skin.

He drew back, still staring at her intently. It was an out-of-body experience as he swept her up into his arms and carried her into the bedroom, easing her onto the lace-draped bed. He dropped his body against hers, his mouth now reconnecting, their tongues danced against each other's.

Catherine felt lost in ecstasy as Noah's fingers teased her throat, caressing her collarbone and each shoulder. Where his fingers led, his mouth and tongue followed, and her skin tingled more and more with each touch. He gently palmed her breasts, and she couldn't begin to remember when he'd loosened her bra. Her nipples blossomed like full, ripe berries, dark chocolate nubs of candy beneath his tongue. His breath was hot and each kiss the gentlest touch. She was writhing with pleasure as he teased her sensibilities, everything about the moment like the sweetest dream come true.

Noah loved her. If Catherine was certain of nothing else, she was certain of that. He loved her with every ounce of his being. Wrapping her arms tightly around him, she knew that every breath, every touch, every kiss, every murmur and tremor through her body was telling.

"I love you, I love you, I love you," she chanted over and over again, the words spun between the soft moans he was eliciting from her. "I love you!"

With an ease and grace that awed her, Noah had stripped the both of them naked, clothes scattered across the floor. Catherine moaned loudly, her skin feeling like she'd been lit on fire. Noah settled himself between her thighs, his member sheathed. He pressed his mouth to her ear, lightly suckling the lobe between his lips, and then he plunged his tongue into the canal and his body into hers, whispering those words back to her.

They made exquisite love, their two bodies moving as one. It was the sweetest give and take, both reveling in each other's touch. The sensations were sweeping and heated until they were drunk with wanting, the need insatiable. They made love, every touch soothing and necessary, the desire so intense that Catherine couldn't imagine ever wanting anyone else. Tears fell from her eyes and from his. Hand in hand, hip-to-hip, mouth to mouth, they took their loving to new heights and it was extraordinary.

He stroked her slowly, over and over again, his

body circling in and out of hers. The intimate dance grew in its intensity, a personal two-step that they were choreographing as they went along. When Noah suddenly cried out with pleasure, wrenching his body hard against hers, the gut-deep sound startled her out of the erotic trance she'd fallen into. He cried out as he fell off the edge of ecstasy, and then she fell with him, orgasmic bliss claiming them both.

The revelry after was a quiet celebration that only they shared. It was slow caresses and easy touches and gentle, sweet kisses. Everything about the two of them together was like the city of Paris: rich, majestic and opulent. Their love a testament to time and a future both were eager to share.

Two days later, Catherine and Noah joined his family for dinner. For the past few days they'd wrapped themselves around each other. Their loving had covered every square inch of the suite, the outdoor terrace and some places that had come as a surprise to them both.

Without a doubt, there wasn't a dimple, mole, birthmark or any strand of hair Catherine wasn't aware of on Noah's body. They had both explored each other's bodies until there was no further flesh to be found. They'd rested in the quiet of each other and had played as if they didn't have a care in the world. Opening the door only to accept the room service they'd ordered, there had been no interest in anything outside the four walls of their room, both totally focused on each other.

The family was all gathered at Le Coq, mentioned as one of their favorite haunts. Le Coq reminded Catherine of an East Village bar in New York City. It was nicely populated space, neither empty nor packed, with several different seating options throughout the room. It had an element of darkness, was a bit dilapidated but it was also sexy and spacious with good music. Catherine imagined it would be a great spot to do some serious people watching.

As Catherine and Noah entered the private dining room, a heavy silence fell over the room, everyone turning to stare at them. Catherine could feel her cheeks flush with color, suddenly embarrassed by the attention.

"It's about time you two came up for air," Naomi said as she turned her attention back to an oversized platter of pan-fried poultry livers, hearts, fried wings and spiced *cromesquis* with foie gras.

Everyone in the room laughed heartily.

Noah shook his head. "I didn't ask for comments from the peanut gallery," he said as he pulled out a seat for Catherine. He then took the seat beside her.

On her other side, Katrina leaned in, whispering softly. "I want some of whatever you're giving him," she said, her eyebrows raised. "All my alone time was spent watching Matthew review contracts and sleep."

Catherine laughed as she whispered back, "If I could bottle and sell it I'd make a mint."

Noah could feel his cheeks turning a brilliant shade of red. A line of sweat beaded across his brow.

Mark Stallion slapped him on the back, a wide grin across his face. "Don't pay anyone here any attention." He reached out to punch fists with Nicholas, the two men laughing heartily.

"And we remember when you use to be awkward around beautiful women!" Nathaniel exclaimed, giving him a thumbs up.

Catherine laughed, leaning to kiss his cheek. "You take your bow, baby. Your girl is a very happy woman. Don't pay them any mind."

Noah brushed a hand across his face. "So, how was the fashion show?" he asked changing the subject. He looked around the table, noticing how each of the men suddenly hung their head. He laughed. "Looks like I'm not the only one who missed out!"

"All of you make me sick," Natalie said rolling her eyes. "Not one of you boys showed up for my show. My own husband didn't show up!"

"And it was a beautiful show!" Joanne exclaimed.

Tinjin tried to wrap his arms around his wife's thin shoulders but she pushed him away, glaring at him. "I'm sorry," Tinjin said. "You know I wanted to be there, though, right?"

"You wouldn't like it if I didn't show up tomorrow for your show, would you?" Natalie dropped her hands to her hips as she stared Tinjin down.

Tinjin shook his head. "Don't play, *Natalia!*" he exclaimed, calling her by her professional name. "You're the face of Tinmen International. There would be no show if you didn't show up."

"Ohhh!" Natalie chimed, her expression smug.

Tinjin shook his head. He reached into the breast pocket of his blazer and pulled out a long, velvet box. "Would this make it up to you?" he questioned, passing the gift to her.

A round of ohhs and ahhs rang around the table as Natalie flipped open the lid to expose an eighteen-carat white gold, white sapphire and diamond mesh bracelet.

Natalie squealed with excitement as Tinjin tightened the clasp around her wrist. Throwing her arms around his neck, she kissed his cheek. "Thank you, baby. I love you."

Noah shook his head, a wry grin on his face as he met the look his brother-in-law tossed over his sister's shoulder.

"Take notes, family," Tinjin exclaimed, a bright smile filling his face. "This is how you make your woman happy."

Catherine couldn't remember ever laughing so hard with her own family, but the Stallions had her doubled over in tears. The love between them was magnanimous, the joy deeply contagious. The teasing and banter between them was only exceeded by the many heartfelt moments of endearment that only loved ones understood.

They closed the doors to the restaurant, John and his brothers buying an extra two hours of the staff's time. As they stood to leave, Natalie waved her hands excitedly.

"Okay, everybody. And this is for you two specifically," she said pointing a finger at her and Noah.

"We pull out at exactly nine-thirty tomorrow morning so please be in the lobby by nine-fifteen. The bus is going to take us to the Eiffel Tower for a family photo shoot then we're heading to the Carrousel du Louvre for the show. So I really need everyone to show up on time, and Noah—" she narrowed her gaze on her brother "—I need you and Catherine to just show up. None of that monkey business you two have been pulling for the past two days."

Noah tossed up his hands in jest. "I thought I was the big brother? I'm the one who gives orders, not takes them."

John laughed as he tossed an arm around his baby sister's shoulder. "It happens to the best of us. They grow up and suddenly we don't know anything. Isn't that right, Phaedra?"

His sister laughed. "Do what you need to do, girl," she said, eyeballing Natalie. "They'll get over it."

Catherine laughed. "No worries, Natalie. I promise we'll be there on time."

As they all exited the building, climbing into their chauffeured vehicles, Noah winked at his sister and she smiled at him.

Catherine was sleeping soundly when Noah's cell phone vibrated for his attention. He'd been up for over an hour, waiting on the call that signaled for him to go down to the lobby. Crossing the floor on his tiptoes, he carried his shoes in his hand, waiting until he'd closed the suite's door behind him to put them on.

Minutes later, he sat anxiously waiting, nervous energy reeling with a vengeance. As the limousine pulled up in front of the building, he stood, the concierge tossing him an easy smile as he waved.

Charles and Hazel Moore looked travel-weary but excited as they stepped through the hotel's doors. Their son, Charles Moore Jr., nicknamed CJ, followed on their heels. They were a distinguished family and their resemblance to each other ran deep. Catherine had her mother's good looks, but her complexion was all her father's. Despite the difference in their ages, CJ and Catherine could have easily passed for twins.

Catherine had called her younger brother her mother's change-of-life baby, the boy born when she'd been fifteen. Apparently starting over had come with some challenges and the now nineteen-year-old was spoiled, exuding an air of entitlement that his sister frequently threatened to slap out of him.

Noah recognized the family immediately. Although he had never told Catherine, he had met her father many years ago, on the day his own father had turned him away. Back then the Moore family had been members of Reverend Perry's congregation and the two men had been friends. Mr. Moore had been in the church office. Noah, sixteen years old then, had asked for a minute of his father's time, hoping to convince the wayward pastor to acknowledge his illegitimate children and give their mother a much needed hand.

Reverend Perry had been less that welcoming, telling Noah to never darken his doorstep ever again. Charles Moore had been kinder, giving Noah advice that he'd followed ever since. Noah paused for a brief moment as he thought back to Catherine's father's words.

"Don't beat yourself up asking why a man doesn't do what he should do. Just remember that good or bad, God will always know that man's heart. And you can't make someone love you, son. So learn to love yourself, keep God first and grow to be the man your mother knows you can be."

But Noah had been angry at both men for months afterward. It wasn't until many years later that he could appreciate Mr. Moore's timely advice.

He took a deep breath as he extended his hand. "Mr. Moore, Mrs. Moore, I'm Noah Stallion."

Catherine's father hesitated for a brief second, or at least Noah thought so.

"Noah, it's a pleasure," Catherine's mother said, pulling him into a warm embrace. "We've heard such good things about you."

"It's been some years, young man. It's good to see you again," Mr. Moore said.

CJ nodded his head but said nothing as he continued to bob his head to the music that played on the earphones connected to his iPod.

"I hope your trip was satisfactory?"

Mrs. Moore nodded. "It was. We couldn't have asked for better." She looked past his shoulder and around the room. "Where is that daughter of ours?"

Noah smiled. "She was sound asleep. And she doesn't know you're here. She has no idea that I called and invited you to come to Paris."

Her parents exchanged a look, both eyeing him curiously.

"I can explain," Noah said, "but why don't I show you both to your room first. Catherine might come looking for me, and I don't want to spoil the surprise."

Minutes later, Noah had the family comfortably ensconced in a two-bedroom suite on another floor of the hotel. CJ fell across the living room's sofa, still listening to his music. Charles Sr. rolled his eyes in annoyance, snatching the earplugs from his hands.

"Hey, whatcha do that for?" the boy snapped.

"You need to go get a shower and change," Mr. Moore admonished. "We have a schedule to keep and I will not put up with any of your nonsense on this trip. Is that understood?"

"Yeah, whatever," CJ muttered as he stuck the earplugs back into his ears.

"CJ, do what your father says please."

For a brief moment, Noah stood watching as the parents went back and forth with their son, the boy intent on doing what he wanted and not what he was asked. After CJ had finally retreated into the other room, the couple took a seat, gesturing for Noah to do the same.

"So why don't you tell us what's going on?" Mrs. Moore said.

Noah took a deep breath. "I don't know what Catherine has told you about me or about us but your daughter and I have become very close."

Mrs. Moore smiled. She reached for her husband's hand, squeezing it gently.

"You two haven't known each other long, have you?" her father asked.

"Well…it's only been a few months since our high school reunion when we reconnected."

"That's right. I forgot that you two went to high school together."

Mrs. Moore giggled softly. "You probably don't know it, but Catherine had the biggest crush on you in high school."

Noah smiled. "Probably not as big as my crush on her, Mrs. Moore." He shifted forward in his seat, clasping his hands tightly together in front of himself. He took a deep breath.

"Mr. Moore, Mrs. Moore. I love your daughter. And I asked you to come to Paris because I plan to ask her to be my wife. But I knew I couldn't do that until I spoke to the both of you and asked for your blessing. I know how much Catherine respects you and how important it is to her to have your approval. So I guess what I'm trying to say is I'm here to plead my case and if necessary, convince you that I'm the man for your daughter. To let you know just how much I love and appreciate her."

Mrs. Moore looked to her husband, fighting to contain her excitement. Mr. Moore leaned back in his seat, pulling one leg over the other. For a brief moment he seemed to be lost in thought until he lifted his eyes back to Noah, meeting his stare.

"We were sorry to hear about your mother's passing, Noah. She was a good woman."

"Thank you, sir. I appreciate that."

"I'm sure you made her very proud."

Noah nodded. "I tried, sir."

"One day, Noah, you might have a daughter of your own and you'll understand how I'm feeling right now. A man doesn't like the idea of giving his daughter away to another man." He paused, the silence becoming a bit uncomfortable before he spoke again. "Even if he is a good and decent man.

"Cat is my baby girl so I only want the very best for her. I know she can take care of herself. But I also know she needs a companion and partner who'll be able to step up to the plate if she ever needs him."

Noah nodded. "Mr. Moore, I assure you that Catherine will be in good hands. As long as I'm able she will want for absolutely nothing."

Mr. Moore stood up, moving onto his feet. Noah stood with him. "I've always trusted my daughter's judgment. You don't accomplish what she's been able to accomplish without making good decisions. From what she's told her mother about you, Mr. Stallion, it seems that she feels for you the same way you feel for her. A father can't fight love like that."

He extended his hand. "Congratulations. My wife and I are delighted to give you our blessing. Do right by my daughter and I'm sure you and I will get along famously."

Noah grinned as his future father-in-law pumped his arm up and down eagerly. "Thank you, sir. Thank you very much."

Mrs. Moore clapped her hands excitedly. "I guess we should go get ready."

Noah stole a quick look at his watch. "My sister will come for you in about two hours. I plan to pop the question at the Eiffel Tower this morning. Catherine won't know you're there until we get to the top."

Mrs. Moore reached up to kiss his cheek. "This is so exciting!"

After they closed the door on his exit, Noah stood for a quick moment outside their room door. He grinned, excitement painting his expression as he pumped a fist in the air, jubilation guiding his steps.

Chapter 14

As Noah moved back through the front lobby he checked off one more item on his mental checklist. The parents, the ideal place, the perfect woman. The last thing he needed to make sure of was the ring. As if on cue, Naomi called his name. She was waiting where Noah had just been sitting before the arrival of Catherine's family.

"Good morning," he said, whispering loudly. He leaned to kiss her cheek as he dropped down onto the seat beside her.

"Does Catherine suspect anything?" Naomi asked.

Noah shook his head. "I don't think so. You did pick that package up for me, didn't you?"

A hint of annoyance crossed his sister's face. "Did

you really think I'd forget to pick up your engagement ring?"

"Of course not, Naomi. I'm just nervous."

"You should be. This is a big step."

He nodded. "I just spoke with her parents and got
their blessing."

"Look at you being all proper and upstanding,
talking to her daddy and asking for her hand."

"It was the right thing to do, right?"

Naomi laughed. "You are nervous!" she exclaimed.

He rolled his eyes.

His sister wrapped an arm around his shoulder
and gave him a quick hug. "For what it's worth we
all really like her. Even Natalie, and you know she
doesn't like anyone. Catherine is perfect for you. I
personally look forward to spending some time with
her and getting to know her even better."

Noah smiled, leaning to kiss his sister's cheek.
"Thanks. I really needed that."

Naomi nodded. "You need to go get ready. I'll
take care of your in-laws, and stop worrying so
much. It's going to be absolutely perfect."

Back in the room, Catherine was awake, sitting
on the red velvet sofa waiting for him. "You forgot
your cell phone," she said in greeting as he stepped
through the door.

His eyes widened as she continued.

"I tried to call you to see where you were and it
rang. It was under the covers in the bed."

The device now rested on the coffee table in front

of her. Catherine shifted forward in her seat, drawing her hands together as if in prayer. "Who's Sugar and why did she call you this morning? In fact, you two have spoken to each other quite a lot in the past few weeks."

Noah bit back a smile. He took a deep breath, not wanting to show any emotion. "You went through my phone?" he questioned, his brow lifted.

She met his stare with her own. "Do you have something you're hiding from me?"

Noah chuckled softly. "No, I don't, so why would you go through my phone?"

"Then who is Sugar?"

"She's a friend."

"Is that where you went? To meet your *friend*? Because her text message told you to come to the lobby."

Noah didn't miss her intonation on the word *friend*. He laughed. "Catherine Moore, are you that type of woman?"

He saw her visibly bristle, which made him laugh even more.

"What type of woman is that?" she snapped.

"Confident and assured on the outside but secretly insecure and jealous on the inside?"

"I am *not* insecure and I am *definitely* not jealous!" she quipped, her voice rising ever so slightly.

"That's good to know," Noah said with a quick nod. He moved to her side and kissed her forehead, his hands pressed firmly against her shoulders. "We need to get dressed or we're going to be late and I still need to get a shower," he said.

As he stepped away he reached for his cell phone then he disappeared into the other room.

Sugar.

Noah had conveniently avoided answering her questions about who Sugar was and what she was to him. But Catherine had seen enough to know whoever Sugar was, she and Noah were obviously close. A text message exchange that had ended with Noah telling Sugar he loved her and Sugar responding that she loved him more had told Catherine that.

So who the hell was Sugar?

Catherine tilted her face into the spray of water, the shower just warm enough. She suddenly thought about Noah's question. *Was she that kind of woman?* Because truth be told, after going through his phone she was suddenly feeling out of sorts. She had never before imagined herself ever going through her man's phone as if she didn't trust him. And she did trust Noah. She trusted him explicitly. But when her call had given her access to his device, curiosity had gotten the best of her.

She sighed, air escaping past her lips. She should have known better. Wasn't it her friend Camille who'd told her once that if a woman went looking for something wrong in her relationship that she would be sure to find it? Or was that Crystal adding that trusting a man was overrated? She sighed again.

Catherine wanted to just let it go and move past

it but she needed to know more about Sugar. Noah not volunteering to give her answers suddenly had her asking questions she never imagined herself asking. What was the nature of their relationship and just how much love did the two have between them?

A knock on the bathroom door made her jump, the harsh rap pulling her from her thoughts. She was slightly surprised when Noah stuck his head into the room.

"Hey, are you going to be much longer? It's almost nine o'clock."

"No, I'm getting out now," she said as she shut off the raining water.

"Okay. Well, unless you need me to wait for you I think I'll head downstairs. I need to speak with my sister."

She nodded. "That's fine. I won't be long."

There was a moment of pause, the tension between them feeling awkward.

"I love you, Cat," Noah said softly.

She nodded, tears suddenly swelling behind her eyelids. "I love you, too, Noah," she answered.

After he'd closed the door, she slid back the shower curtain, taking one breath and then another. As she stepped out of the claw-foot tub, she muttered under her breath, "I'm still going to find out who Sugar is!"

As the Stallion and Boudreaux family exited the tour bus, Cat moved off to the side, standing alone as she stared at the sky. She was stunning, dressed in a black unitard, black leather boots, and a black leather trench coat. She wore a patterned scarf wrapped loosely around her neck and carried an oversized Coach bag. Her makeup was pristine, her lips shimmering in candy-apple red.

Noah wanted to kiss her candy-colored lips but he knew Catherine wasn't happy with him. He continued to eye her as Marah and Joanne moved to her side, pulling her into conversation. He sensed they were talking about him when both turned in his direction, neither looking happy.

His brothers suddenly distracted him. "Hey, is everything okay?" Nick questioned.

Noah nodded, shifting his gaze away from Catherine.

"Everything's good."

"Your girl looks upset this morning. What did you do?" Nathaniel asked.

Noah laughed. He gave them the short version of his *Sugar* dilemma. The trio laughed heartily together.

"That's why I plan to stay single," Nathaniel intoned. "I can avoid that kind of drama."

"All women bring drama!" Mark interjected, joining the conversation. "They can't help themselves."

"Who are we talking about?" Kendrick Boudreaux asked, extending his hand to the group in greeting.

Everyone turned to acknowledge the family that had just arrived on the second tour bus. Kendrick was joined by his wife, Vanessa, his sister Maitlyn and her husband, Zakaria Sayed. His brother Donovan and his sisters, Kamaya and Tarah, his brother Guy and Guy's wife, Dahlia, Darryl and his wife, Camryn, and their parents weren't too far behind. The hugs and kisses were abundant as the two families reconnected.

Natalie suddenly gestured for everyone's attention, shouting out instructions. Arrangements had been made to enable them to bypass the notoriously long lines to climb the monument. The family and a team of photographers were guided through a special entrance to the elevators that took them right to the summit.

As the family took turns entering the elevators Noah moved to Catherine's side and grabbed her hand. She tensed for a brief second before relaxing into his touch.

"You still mad at me?" Noah questioned, his voice a low whisper.

"I was never mad."

He laughed. "Oh, yes, you were!"

"No. I wasn't. I was just curious about your *friend*."

There was that intonation again, Catherine spitting the word out as if it were bitter in her mouth. He shook his head. "That woman doesn't mean anything to me."

"If you say so."

"I do."

The tour guide gestured for them to wait, the lift too full to take on anyone else. Noah, Catherine and the photographer were suddenly the last ones waiting to go to the top.

Noah turned and grabbed her hands. "Do you trust me, Catherine?" he asked, calling her by her full name. "And I really want you to think about that before you answer. Do you, Catherine Moore, trust me?"

She gazed into his eyes, his soulful stare rippling heat into the pit of her stomach. "Of course I do. I love you."

"Then why are you questioning something as irrelevant as me having a conversation with another woman? Obviously if it were important I would tell you. But it's not. It doesn't impact how I feel about you or how you feel about me so why are you getting so worked up?"

She shrugged. "I just... Well...I..." she stammered, unable to formulate an answer that would actually make sense.

Noah pulled her close and kissed her. As his mouth met hers she suddenly realized just how foolish she'd been. She smiled, the tension falling from her face.

"I'm sorry," she apologized. "I don't know what got into me."

Noah nodded. "Me, either, but you definitely have a little jealous streak. That surprised me."

"It surprised me, too, and I see that I'm a little possessive. I was really having a hard time thinking that Sugar might have a piece of your heart that I didn't have."

He laughed. "Trust me when I tell you that no other woman has my heart the way you have my heart."

Catherine nodded, her smile bright. "So who names their child Sugar, anyway?"

Before either could comment further, the elevator doors opened and the couple were ushered inside. The ride was quick and when the door reopened both were suddenly struck by the panoramic views of the city below. As Catherine stepped out of the conveyor she was transfixed on the sights, not noticing the family that stood grinning with excitement.

"It's so beautiful!" she exclaimed, tossing Noah a look over her shoulder.

He smiled back. "Yes, you are!"

"I can't believe…" she started when she turned and caught sight of her parents beaming happily at her.

She eyed them briefly before fixing her eyes on Noah and back. "Daddy? Mom? What are you…?" Catherine turned again, suddenly aware of everyone staring at her. It was only then that she noticed that Noah had dropped to one knee in front of her, his hands extended, a small black velvet box resting in his palms.

She clasped her hand over her mouth, her eyes wide with shock. Out of nowhere a trio of stringed instruments began to play Vivaldi, the music billowing with the breeze that gusted around them. Tears burned hot behind her lids beginning to rain down over her cheeks.

Noah took a glance around to his family and friends, a smile pulling at his full lips. Both his sisters were fighting back tears, and joy shone over everyone's faces. He turned back to Catherine and his heart was suddenly full.

"Catherine, I am amazed at how quickly our friendship caught fire. You have become everything to me and having you by my side is what completes me. As I think about my future I can't imagine a life without you in it. Will you please do me the honor of being my wife?" He pulled an impressive diamond ring from the box and slipped it onto her ring finger. He lifted his gaze to hers, anxiously awaiting her answer.

"Yes! Yes! Yes!" Catherine squealed as she threw her arms around Noah's neck, hugging him tightly. "Oh, yes!" She laughed as she kissed him.

Lifting her into his arms, Noah spun her around, their excitement spilling over as their families applauded and cheered. They were suddenly surrounded, everyone wanting to offer their congratulations.

Mr. Moore shook Noah's hand and his brothers both gave him a one armed embrace, bringing him in close. He watched as Catherine and her mother hugged each other, both jumping up and down excitedly. His sisters and cousins kissed and hugged the both of them and the photographers captured it all for posterity.

The rest of the day was a blur. The family had moved from the Eiffel Tower to the Parisian runway where Tinjin and Natalie formally introduced his newest collection of men's wear for women. It was a cornucopia of meticulously tailored slacks, luxurious blouses in satins and silks and fitted jackets and blazers that easily transitioned from daywear to nightwear. The impressive pieces were paired with shoe designs, and most of the women in the family went crazy, wanting to order everything they could see.

Dinner was a family feast complete with reunion-style T-shirts designed by Tinjin and Natalie. Everyone was there to celebrate and the children ran back and forth through the banquet space at the hotel. The noise was abundant with laughter.

Noah and Catherine sat side-by-side, his arms wrapped warmly around her. She pointed across the room. "Okay, who's the little girl in the plaid dress and red boots?"

Noah turned to look where she stared. "That's Mark and Michelle's daughter. Her name's Irene. And the little girl standing beside her is John and Marah's baby."

"Gabi, right?"

He nodded. "That's right."

"And the boy standing with my brother?"

"That's Matthew and Katrina's son, Collin. Collin and CJ are probably about the same age."

"And all the little babies!" she exclaimed. "How can you keep up with them all?"

Noah laughed. "That's what my sisters are for." He waved a hand at Naomi, gesturing for her attention.

"What's up?" she asked, dropping into a seat on the other side of the table.

"Catherine wants to know who all the babies are and I can't tell her."

Naomi laughed. She turned to look around the room then pointed her finger. "The little girl your mother is cuddling is Darryl and Camryn Boudreaux's baby girl, Alexa. You know who Darryl and Camryn are, right?"

Catherine nodded. "Darryl is Kendrick, Mason and Katrina's brother."

"And the two babies toddling about over there are their brother Guy's twins, Sydney and Cicely. Their mother is Dahlia."

"Dahlia's the filmmaker and Camryn is an architect?"

"You got it! Did I miss anyone?"

The two women looked about the room. Catherine pointed toward a little boy trying his hardest to sit atop a rubber ball. "Who's that little guy?"

"That's Jacoby. He's Matthew and Katrina's youngest son."

"Oh, and don't forget Lorenzo and Tianna," Noah added. "They're my cousin Travis's kids."

"His wife, Tierra, and Tinjin are sister and brother."

"See, you know everyone," he said.

"So, now that you two are engaged, are you thinking about babies?" Naomi asked, humor dancing in her gaze.

"Don't answer that," Noah said, shooting Catherine a look.

Catherine laughed. "You two are so funny."

Moving onto her feet, Naomi shook her head. "We'll talk later, sister-in-law! When my brother is not around!"

Noah shook his head as Catherine giggled. "Do not talk to my sister," he said. "I'm warning you now."

She nuzzled her face into his neck and pressed a kiss to his cheek.

"Thank you," she said as she extended her hand forward, admiring the diamond on her ring finger.

Noah smiled. "For what?"

"For loving me. This day could not have been more perfect."

Noah kissed her back, allowing his lips to linger until his heart skipped a few beats. As he pulled away, the arrival of another guest caught his eye. Catherine turned to look where he was staring. Noah stood up, grabbing her hand.

"There's someone I want you to meet," he said, pulling her along beside him.

Natalie and Tinjin stood in conversation with the woman. She wore long gray dreadlocks pulled into a bun atop her head. Her warm chocolate complexion clearly belied her age, and she had smiling eyes, Catherine thought. The woman's bohemian spirit was evident in her attire, the floor length, African-print caftan flattering. There was something warm and welcoming about her presence, and Catherine instinctively knew the woman had a nurturing spirit.

"Who is that?" she asked.

Noah tossed her a look and smiled. "That's my other girlfriend," he said sarcastically.

A wave of confusion danced in Catherine's stare. "What?"

Noah laughed as they stepped into the conversation his sister and her husband were having.

The woman greeted him warmly, excitement in her tone. "Mr. Noah! How are you?"

"I'm really good. I just had to come over and thank you for everything you did to help make this day happen for me."

The woman threw her arms around him in a gregarious hug. "I was so glad to be of help. I hear everything went very well."

"It did."

"I wish I could have been there but there was much preparation that had to be done for the fashion show."

"I understand." He slid an arm around Catherine's waist, easing her forward. "I want to introduce you to my fiancée. This is Catherine. Catherine, meet Sugar."

Catherine's eyes widened. "You're Sugar?"

The woman nodded. "I am. It's an old family name. Back in the day I use to tell people it was my stripper name!" she said with a rich, deep cackle.

Natalie laughed. "Sugar works for Tinmen International. She's one of our assistants, and we couldn't have done all of this without her."

Catherine's face flushed a deep shade of red. She was speechless as the older woman pulled her into a warm hug. "Congratulations on your engagement. You've got yourself quite a catch there."

Catherine nodded. "Thank you. Thank you so much."

Natalie looped her arm through Sugar's. "Come, let me introduce you to the rest of the family," she said as she pulled the woman along beside her.

Catherine slid into Noah's outstretched arms. "Okay, I am officially embarrassed. I'm so sorry."

Noah laughed, kissing her cheek. "I would never, ever be unfaithful to you. I hope that you always know you can trust that. That you can trust me."

"I know, and I promise that I will never go through your phone again and jump to conclusions."

"You are welcome to go through my phone anytime. I have nothing I need to hide from you. But if something concerns you all you need to do is ask me."

Minutes later, Noah was laughing heartily with the men on one side of the room and Catherine was holding one of the babies. The women surrounding her offering wedding and marriage advice. Catherine snuggled the child close to her heart and smiled, catching Noah's eye. And he couldn't help but smile back.

The rest of their week was event filled as they played tourist, Noah wanting her to see everything he loved about Paris. They took walks in the Jardins des Tuileries, drank hot chocolate at Angelina on the rue de Rivoli, traveled to the Musée Grévin to see the waxworks, and the Louvre to see the works of art. They admired the gilt dome of the opera house, its majestic cupola painted by Chagall, and took every spare moment to appreciate the opulent architecture throughout the city. Paris was vibrant and intoxicating and the perfect place for their love to bloom.

Catherine actually hated the prospect of leaving but at the end of the week they were back on a plane, headed home. They shared the flight with Noah's brothers—the two men needing to be in New York for Nicholas's game against New York. And for the first time since they'd left the United States, Noah allowed her access to her emails. She sat reading message after message while the three men chatted easily together, reflecting back on their vacation.

"We should do this more often," Nathaniel said. "I can't remember the last time I had so much fun."

Noah concurred. "It was a great time," he said. "It just feels good to connect to our family like that."

Nicholas sighed. "So are you going to tell us about that honey you met up with?" he questioned, his eyes focused on his twin. "Baby girl was tight! I bet you could bounce a quarter off her backside!"

Noah held his hands out. "Really? Is that how you talk about women?"

Nathaniel grinned, cutting a quick eye at Catherine. He leaned in to whisper.

Catherine suddenly cleared her throat, lifting her

gaze to meet his. She shook her head, Nathaniel's foolish expression making her laugh.

The young man lowered his gaze in apology, a contrite smile on his face. "Sorry, Cat, I was just…"

She waved a dismissive hand at him. "Carry on. Don't mind me."

"Let's not." Nathaniel chuckled. He took a sip of the bottled spring water he'd been drinking. "She was one of Natalie's friends and she's a very sweet girl. There's nothing else to tell."

Catherine laughed heartily. "I'm sure. You can tell it when we land," she said. "I promise I'll get right out of your way so you three can talk boy talk without being interrupted."

Noah laughed. "Which means the minute we land you plan to head right over to the office, right?"

She grinned, her face appearing as if she'd been caught with her hand in a cookie jar. "I've been gone for a whole week. No contact whatsoever. I have to go to the office."

Noah shook his head, chuckling softly. "That's my CEO," he said, moving to the seat beside her. He wrapped her in his arms and hugged her tightly.

When the plane touched down at Teterboro Airport, the general aviation terminal for many private aviation charter companies in the New York/New Jersey area, Noah and Catherine both knew they were going to miss his family. The goodbyes were quick and sweet, the twins heading off in their rental car, and Catherine and Noah being picked up by limo. The short ride to midtown took no time at all.

Minutes later the car service pulled up to the doors of Fly High's offices.

There was no missing the excitement across Catherine's face. She'd missed the day-to-day routine that had been about building her empire. The fire and drive had been invigorated with the time she'd had off. The vacation had done her good, and Noah could see her mind racing to figure out her next steps.

"I need to hire a replacement for Frederick," she said. "I was talking to your cousin John about it and he mentioned a few people that he would highly recommend."

Noah smiled. "Don't let it worry you tonight, Cat. You're not going to fill that seat before sunrise."

She laughed. "I am getting ahead of myself, I know. I'm just so excited. We've had record stock sales, the company is getting good press and that horror show that was my former COO hasn't negatively impacted my business. I'm just so ready to move forward and I can't do that until I can hire someone to help me manage the company. Once that's done then I have to focus on planning my wedding." She tossed Noah a look, his head snapping toward her.

"That's right. We have to plan our wedding. I'm not doing that long engagement thing. And we have a ton of decisions to make. We have to decide where we're going to live. What we plan to name our children. It's a long list, Noah."

Noah grinned. "Then I think we should start reviewing employment applications before we go to bed tonight."

Catherine laughed. "That's what I'm saying!"

They entered the building hand in hand. Bishop waved excitedly as he rushed to the glass doors to let them inside.

"Y'all have been missed!" the old man exclaimed. "It wasn't the same without the two of you here!"

"You just made my day," Catherine said as she gave the man a warm hug. "Because we missed you, too."

Noah shook Bishop's hand and bumped his shoulder.

"Anything we need to know about?" Catherine asked.

Bishop shook his head. "No, ma'am. We had that little situation with Mr. Ross but Mr. Stallion handled that. Everything's been good since."

Catherine looked confused, turning to give Noah a look. "What little situation?"

"It was nothing," Noah said, his eyebrows raised as he focused his gaze on Bishop.

Catherine waved an index finger at the two of them. "Uh-uh, not this time! Mr. Bishop, what happened with Mr. Ross?" she asked again, turning to stare directly at the man.

Bishop looked from one to the other. Catherine stared at him intensely. She held a hand up in front of Noah's face. "And do not look at Mr. Stallion."

"Yes, ma'am," Bishop said, fighting to keep from shifting his eyes. "Well, it… He…umm…" the man stammered, suddenly thrown off guard. He twisted his hands nervously.

Catherine shifted her gaze to Noah. "No more shielding me, Noah. I want to know what happened. And I want to know it now." There was a brief moment of silence. "Please."

Noah nodded his head slightly. "Thank you, Mr. Bishop," he said. "I'll take it from here."

Bishop nodded. "Thank you, sir. I need to go make my rounds," he said as he rushed off in the opposite direction.

Catherine turned to face him, her hands holding up her full hips. She tilted her head, waiting patiently for Noah to begin talking.

"Frederick was able to make bail."

"I thought you said they gave him a million-dollar cash bond?"

"They did."

"And he was able to raise that kind of money that quickly?"

"He did, but Kendrick believes he had some help from the cartel that he was apparently helping."

"So he's out?"

Noah shook his head. "He was out but he violated the terms of his bail and is now being held in a maximum security federal prison until his trial."

Catherine squinted her eyes, trying to put the pieces of the story together. "What did he do?" she asked. "To violate his bail."

"He was found trespassing on Fly High property. He snuck into the building, hid in one of the offices until closing and then went to your office. The police believe he was going to try to ambush you. He says he only wanted to talk to you, to explain what happened but he was armed. He just didn't anticipate you not being here since you are always here."

Catherine gasped, drawing a hand to her chest. Her eyes were wide, shock registering across her face. "How...?"

Noah continued, not waiting for her to ask her next question. "Mr. Bishop ran into him while making his rounds. There was a brief altercation but Mr. Bishop was faster with his weapon than Frederick was. The security team moved in and got him into handcuffs without anyone getting hurt. They contacted me while we were in Paris. I was satisfied with how it was handled and that was it."

"Why didn't you tell me? This is my company and you should have told me!" There was a hint of attitude in her tone and the minute the words passed her lips, she felt him stiffen.

Noah stood staring at her, his head bobbing, his eyes skating from side to side as he chose his words carefully. He pulled his shoulders back, straightening his posture. When he finally spoke there was no missing the edge of control in his voice.

"If I had told you, you would have wanted to fly right back here. You would have been worried and you would have agonized over what to do or not do. You would have tried to micromanage the situation and the reality is there was nothing else you could have done. I wanted to climb the Eiffel Tower and I wanted you to climb it with me. So I made an executive decision."

Catherine stood staring at him. In that brief moment she suddenly saw her entire future evolve before her eyes. Everything she had ever wanted, had ever dreamed of, was staring down at her. She only had to embrace it, and it was hers to have. She could relinquish control, step back, follow and not lead, and she could depend on him and trust that if she fell, Noah Stallion would catch her.

She took a deep breath and held it, and then turned and headed in the direction of the front door.

Noah called after her. "I thought you wanted to go to your office?"

She tossed him a look over her shoulder. "I changed my mind," she said. She bit down on her bottom lip, a come-hither look piercing her gaze. "I have something else for us to do."

Noah stood like a statue, surprise creasing his forehead. A slow smiled pulled at his full lips. "I'll let Mr. Bishop know we won't be staying," he said as he reached for the remote radio.

"You do that," Catherine said as she gave him a seductive wink of her eye. "I'll flag us down a cab."

Chapter 15

Noah spent the entire cab ride back to Catherine's apartment thinking about making love to her the entire night. Slow, sweet, hot, passionate love, kissing, holding, touching for the next eight hours.

They sat an arm's length, neither saying a word but the sexual tension was monumental. She sat beside him with her legs slightly askew. She was chewing on the fingers of her left hand, sucking her fingers past her lips, slowly in and out. Her other hand skated from one thigh to the other, teasing the soft flesh. Her breathing was heavy, her breath coming in low, deep pants.

Noah palmed his own hand across his crotch, the gesture quick and brief as he adjusted the length of steel that had hardened in his pants. It took every ounce of his fortitude not to take her right there in the backseat of that taxi. By the time he'd paid the driver, Catherine was already going through the doors of her apartment building, the voluptuous shimmy of her backside beckoning him to her.

The elevator doors were closing as he raced into the building behind her and for a brief moment he contemplated running up the stairs. Instead, he leaned on the elevator buttons, willing it to come back down and come back fast. By the time the conveyor dropped back down to the first floor he felt like he might explode from wanting.

The ride upstairs seemed to take forever. All Noah could think of was losing himself deep inside of her. Then melting beneath the heat of her until he was a mere semblance of himself, Catherine claiming every ounce of his being. Once inside the penthouse apartment, he tossed his jacket aside and kicked off his shoes. A wide smile blossomed across his face as he followed the trail of clothes that led him to her.

She'd done a striptease from the front door to the bedroom, leaving her coat and high heels in the foyer. Her blouse and slacks lay puddled down the length of hallway. Her panties rested at the bedroom door and her lace bra hung on the doorknob. Noah inhaled two deep breaths before he turned the latch and pushed the door open.

Catherine lay atop the mattress, the bedding snatched to the floor, a pile of pillows propped behind her head. Her legs were crossed at the ankles, her arms were folded over her chest, and she twisted strands of pearls between her lips. Noah's body began to tingle with a vengeance, the wealth of it a volcanic mass between his legs. By the time he made it to the side of the bed he'd stripped out of the last of his own clothes, standing naked before her, a condom covering the length of steel between his legs.

Reaching out his arm, Noah placed the palm of his hand against her face, his fingers gently caressing her soft flesh. Lifting one knee onto the mattress and then the other, he gazed into her eyes and whispered her name over and over again.

"I love you, Cat," he said just before he leaned forward and pressed his mouth to hers. He pulled her closer as their lips danced together, their tongues meeting and playing gently together. The kiss was warm and delightful as his hands slid into her hair, his tongue delving deeper as their connection intensified.

He felt possessed as he sucked and nibbled and tasted her mouth, his body dropping down against hers. He held her tight as he pressed her down against the mattress top, his chest kissing the round of her breasts, his hands sliding down her back to clutch the curves of her bottom.

He felt his body spasm as she slid one leg up against his, sliding it and then the other around his back. His mouth moved to her neck, nuzzling, kissing and suckling the soft tissue, his hands still squeezing and rubbing her skin. He licked her earlobe and whispered into her ear, "I love you, Cat."

Catherine inhaled sharply and moaned the words

back as he hit her sweet spot, the intensity of his touch setting her afire. He licked her neck then covered her breasts with his mouth. He sucked each nipple, swirling circles with his tongue as the chocolate nubs hardened beneath his teeth.

His body eased down the length of hers, his hands dancing across her belly, his tongue teasing the well of her belly button. Her skin was hot, the heat raising his own temperature. She trembled and he trembled with her, every fiber of his being quivering with desire as he kissed his way down to her mound.

The intimate kiss had her writhing with pleasure, her body feeling like it was about to implode. He kissed, licked and sucked until she was tottering at the edge of pleasure. His touch was hedonistic, his kisses carnal and indulgent, and then he moved back up her body as if he intended to start all over again.

Catherine's breathing was static as she gasped for air, panting heavily. Moisture puddled between her thighs and breasts, perspiration showering her skin. His touch was intoxicating, and she was drunk with desire, a feeling she'd never known.

Noah rose up on his forearms to stare down at her. "Open your eyes," he said, his soft tone commanding. And she did, meeting his intoxicating stare.

Everything either needed was in the other's gaze. The wanting, the intensity, the promise. The magnitude of their connection moving them both to tears. Noah tilted his face into the palm of her hand as she brushed the saline from his cheek.

"I love you!" he exclaimed again, the words catch-

ing deep in his chest as he plunged his body into hers.
And it was the echo of those same words out of Catherine's mouth that fueled his intensity as he thrust
his body hard against hers, their eyes still locked
tightly together.

The moment was magic as his body dissolved into
hers, his hardened muscles melting like molten lava
against her touch. She welcomed him in, the walls
of her feminine spirit embracing him. His touch
was soul deep, her muscles drawing him deeper and
deeper until she cried out, chanting the same mantra
he did. "Oh, Noah, baby! I love you, too!"

They orgasmed together. Both their bodies tens-
ing, everything seeming to stop for a second. And
then it hit, the explosion magnanimous, the shock
waves raging from head to toe. Together they rode
the waves together, clinging tightly to each other.
And for the rest of the night, Noah worked that Stallion magic over and over again, every dream in his
heart come true.

"You actually took a vacation?" Camille questioned, disbelief ringing in her voice.

Catherine smiled into her cell phone as if her best
friend could see her. "I did. Noah took me to Paris
for the week."

"Noah Stallion took you to Paris, and you actually went?"

"Why do you say it like that?"

"I'm just trying to figure out what kind of voodoo
that man worked on you."

"Really, Camille?"

"I'm just saying."

"Did you get my text message? I sent you a picture."

"Hold on," Camille said. "You know I can't walk and chew gum at the same time. My belly's too big."

"That's why we have the latest and greatest technology. Look at your text."

"Hold on," Camille said, the phone fumbling in her hand.

Catherine heard her friend gasp, then scream loudly on the other end. She laughed hysterically.

"Is that a ring on your hand?"

Catherine giggled.

"You're engaged?"

"Yes, I am marrying Noah Stallion!" she exclaimed excitedly, telling the story of how he'd proposed.

"Unbelievable!"

"It was magical!"

Noah suddenly stood in the doorway, having found the bed empty and cold. A hint of sleep still teased his eyes. His expression was questioning. Catherine grinned, her smile bright.

"Call me later, Camille," she said. "I need to handle some business."

Camille laughed. "So what else is new?" she said facetiously. "Some things never change."

"Goodbye, Camille."

As Catherine disconnected the call, she locked eyes with Noah.

"What's on our agenda today?" he asked, rubbing at his eyes with the backs of his hands.

Catherine eased to his side, wrapping her arms around his waist as she settled her naked body against his.

"Us, baby! Nothing but us!"

* * * * *

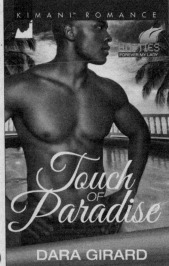

REQUEST YOUR FREE BOOKS!

2 FREE NOVELS
PLUS 2 FREE GIFTS!

KIMANI™
ROMANCE

Love's ultimate destination!